Paradox

Paradox

S. Hale Humphrey-Jones, Ph.D.

Paradox

Copyright © 2024 by S. Hale Humphrey-Jones, Ph.D. All rights reserved.

No part of this publication may be reproduced, stored in a retrieval system or transmitted in any way by any means, electronic, mechanical, photocopy, recording or otherwise without the prior permission of the author except as provided by USA copyright law.

The opinions expressed by the author are not necessarily those of URLink Print and Media.

1603 Capitol Ave., Suite 310 Cheyenne, Wyoming USA 82001
1-888-980-6523 | admin@urlinkpublishing.com

URLink Print and Media is committed to excellence in the publishing industry.

Book design copyright © 2024 by URLink Print and Media. All rights reserved.

Published in the United States of America

Library of Congress Control Number: 2024912505
ISBN 978-1-68486-817-9 (Paperback)
ISBN 978-1-68486-820-9 (Digital)

15.05.24

INTRODUCTION

How many times in our lives do we ask ourselves, "What would I do if?" We know (or at least believe) we have the best of intentions. We would never hurt anyone—at least not on purpose. Of course, we know there are evil people out there who care only for themselves and would not hesitate to do harm—or worse—but do we really know who they are?

We used to be able to differentiate the good guys from the bad by the color of their hats. In the Old West, the good guys wore white hats, the bad guys wore dark.

We remember watching the dark hats sporting downturned mustaches and riding into town to wreak havoc—a memorable motion picture accompanied with ominous music. We were prepared to dislike them every single time.

The white hats saved the day, leading the charge as we knew they would.

Life was simpler then.

Disillusionment occurred when we discovered that those who were supposed to be good do bad things; the white hats did not always save the day. The *perfect* husband was actually a wife abuser. Clergy, teachers, and coaches committed unspeakable acts of abuse on those who trusted them. Sports heroes cheated. Our revered leaders lied. Respected members of the community were sometimes serial killers, and rapists looked like Ted Bundy.

Who should we trust?

Good people sometimes do bad things resulting from illness or addiction. They may actually delude themselves into thinking that their acts are sanctioned by God, or that they are aiding society in some way.

Sometimes the *bad* do good things, confusing us even more. The convicted felon saves a child from drowning. The gang member becomes a neighborhood organizer. The drug addict becomes a counselor.

No longer is it is easy to tell the good guys from the bad guys. The hats are often gray. People, it might seem, are a *paradox*.

Many of my books are based on true experiences.

PROLOGUE

Tonight! He was coming for her tonight. Deirdre woke with the certainty that this would be the night that he would try to kill her. She thought she should be afraid, but an eerie calm feeling came over her at the realization that tonight it would be over at last. One way or another, it would all end.

There were many loose ends that needed to be completed, and Deirdre spent the day finishing notes and paperwork. She also finalized her will and e-mailed it to her attorney for safekeeping—just in case.

As dusk fell, she began the preparations for what was to come. She turned off her phone, sending the calls directly to voice mail. She wanted none of her loved ones to be involved.

Walking from room to room, Deirdre pulled all the drapes closed. Leaving one lamp on in her bedroom, she took down the weapon from the wall safe in the closet and began turning off all the other lights in the house. As darkness fell in earnest, she moved into the living room, slipping into her favorite armchair.

Facing the door, she felt the gun resting harmlessly in her lap. The weapon was still in its box, but loaded, so perhaps not so harmless after all. Shadows fell on the door and the chair next to it. Somehow she knew he would come through the front door. He was that brazen. No sneaking through the basement for him. Calmly, she watched the door and waited for him to come.

DEIRDRE

The sudden shrill sound startled Deirdre so much that the coffee in her hand slopped onto her notes. In a sudden flurry of clumsiness, as she attempted to right the cup, her pen flew across the room and papers scattered everywhere.

"It's just a phone," she told herself. "What's wrong with you?"

A voice deeper inside of her warned, "Don't answer it."

Could there be such a thing as a bad news ring? God, she must be getting paranoid. All morning Deirdre had felt restless and uneasy. Every sound issued a warning no matter how insignificant. A flutter of the window shade, a rattle of papers, a purr from the cat, all initiated an acceleration of her heart and sweating of her palms. Such anxiety was unlike her.

Deirdre's morning routine consisted of returning phone calls to clients from her home office, completing forms for insurance companies, and drinking several cups of coffee (perhaps that was the problem).

No, there wasn't any particular reason for the feeling, which concerned her even more.

Well, except for those phone calls she'd been getting.

Everyone gets those calls though, she reasoned.

They hang up after a minute.

Probably kids playing jokes or wrong numbers. Nothing to worry about. Don't be silly.

Yet from the moment she awakened this morning, she kept hearing a warning. *Be careful.*

Don't be such a baby, she chastised herself as she could hear her Nana saying, "Dee, it's just a phone."

Shaking her head, she reached for the persistent instrument.

Taking a deep breath she answered, "Dr Warren."

(Did her voice quaver just a bit?)

"Dee? You sound weird. Is that you?"

"Karol?" Deirdre laughed with relief. "It's so good to hear your voice. God, I haven't talked to you in weeks. When are we having lunch?"

There was silence on the other end for a few seconds before Karol responded. "Dee, I have some news."

Deirdre shook her head in denial. Karol's tone told her this was not going to be happy news.

"Sure, okay, let's get together and catch up. I can hear all the news at once."

"No, Dee, this can't wait."

Deirdre started to chatter again, but Karol interrupted suddenly. "Dee, he's getting out. They're letting Jack out any day now. Actually, he could be out now Dee, did you hear me? Are you still there?"

Deirdre sighed deeply, holding the phone against her chest before she responded.

"I'm here, Karol. I think I've been expecting it. In fact, I called the court and asked about getting a restraining order, but they said that I had no grounds unless he began harassing me."

"After everything he did to you, everything you've been through, you have no grounds? Dee, you lost your license because of him, you nearly lost your life."

"I know, I know. I was angry when they told me they were releasing him, but they said as soon as he contacts me, and I ask him not to call again, then I can file the order, but not before. It does make sense, Karol. He has rights, too."

"Rights? He has the right to hire someone to kill you, to steal your clients' money and leave you broke and your reputation in ruins?"

"Hey. This is me. I was there remember? You don't need to remind me what he did. How did you find out so soon?"

"I have a friend in the Justice Department. He saw it come through the computer system. He said someone would probably notify you, but I didn't want to take a chance. I thought you'd want to know ASAP."

"Thanks, Karol. You've been a great friend through all of this. I don't know what I would have done without you."

"Just watch your back, friend. I don't want to read about you in the paper,"

Hanging up the phone, Deirdre stared into the stream of coffee covering her desk and began methodically sopping it up with a paper towel. Then suddenly she picked the cup and hurled it across the room, frightening her cat, Pax, who hissed and scurried into the loft to hide. "Why can't this ever end?"

The fury was spent as soon as it began, and Deirdre laughed at herself as she began cleaning up the additional mess, cradling her beloved, but now chipped *View* mug. The mug was one of the very few gifts she'd accepted from clients. She'd patiently explained over and over that she was not allowed to accept gifts from clients unless it was something she could share, such as cookies.

The *View*, however, was the one concession she made to watching daytime television. Deirdre didn't begin office hours until after one, working until late in the evening. She made the one-hour talk show her early lunch break, loving the strong, opinionated women who bantered over current events and issues. Sometimes she referred to the show when talking to clients. It was part of her attempt to relax them and build rapport.

The woman who gave her the mug was being discharged, having met her goals and doing remarkably well. She asked if she could give her the mug as a parting gift. Deirdre didn't have the heart to tell her no. Now she'd managed to chip her favorite mug in a fit of anger. How childish! The pain always seemed to be resurrected when Jack was propelled back into her life.

Recovering from the damage her ex-husband, Jack Stiles, had inflicted had taken five years and had been slow and agonizing. The board had finally reinstated her license a year ago, allowing her to return to her private psychotherapy practice. Last week, she had written the final check paying off the credit cards and bills he had run up before he was arrested.

Every time she began to think the horror was over, something happened to take her back there. She would relive the agony of seeing her husband taken off in handcuffs and remember the horror of being told how he had taken money from her clients. Most of all, she recalled the shame and public humiliation when many believed she was involved in his actions.

She was so beaten down she couldn't even defend herself when the board of regulations took her license. There was no money to hire an attorney, and she was in such a state of shock that she had no defense. The first year was one of basic survival as she lost her income, her reputation, and nearly her life. After that, she began the long, agonizing process of rebuilding and recovering. And she thought she had recovered—until now.

She would not let him destroy her. He had nearly done so before. She wouldn't let it happen now She wondered if Hawke knew Jack was getting out. Probably. Hawke knew everything. She shivered as she remembered the first time she had met the very strange black-haired man with the very surprising soft voice.

"They call me Hawke. I might s well tell you that I came here to kill you."

Hawke had called Deirdre when Jack had been in prison six months, shortly after their divorce had became final. He said he wanted to pick up a book for him, a poetry book. Jack was always asking favors of men who had been released, many of them requesting items to take to him. So Deirdre wasn't surprised at the request and easily agreed to give him the book. An hour later, he shocked her with his revelation.

"Relax, miss, I said I came here to kill you, but I changed my mind. If I hadn't, you'd be dead by now."

Deidre was too shocked to ask. She tried, but her throat was so dry with fear the words wouldn't come out. She merely flopped on the couch, shaking in shock, Pax had hidden under the sofa the moment Hawke entered the room

"That husband of yours does not mean you well. He's too much of a coward to do anything on his own. He'll get someone else to do it. Just watch yourself."

"Why?" She finally blurted out. *"Why did you change your mind?"*

"I never actually told him I'd to it. Just let him think I would. And I might have. He helped me with some legal paperwork, and I owe him. But guys like him turn my stomach. He pretends to be so perfect and great. He thinks he's smarter than me. Hah. He doesn't know a thing about me. Naw, I think I'll let him suffer a bit. Just watch out okay?"

Over the past few years, Deidre had come to know Hawke pretty well. She had n o delusions about him, He was clearly a psychopath and was only walking the streets due to a legal technicality; however, contrary to all the literature on psychopaths, Hawke did form allegiances. He liked Deirdre, and they were as close to being friends as he was capable. Still, she always had the feeling that he could change without warning. Her friendship with him was always with clear-cut boundaries and a certain amount of healthy fear.

Now what was she going to do about Jack? Would he contact her, threaten her?

Were all those hung up calls from him?

Stop it, Deirdre, she cautioned herself. You need to get yourself together. She put the notes back in their respective folder. She didn't think she'd get much more done today. Maybe she should call Hawke.

HAWKE

Hawke was a killer. He was also, according to diagnostic criteria, a psychopath. The primary difference, however, was that Hawke didn't enjoy killing. Hawke killed with a chilling absence of any emotion whatsoever. His purpose was always pragmatic, but never mercenary. Consequently, he was not a hired killer, as most thought. Nor did he kill with frequency or abandon. Hawke selected his victims for reasons that only he could ever understand. The one element that made Hawke dangerous was that he was completely void of fear, fear of getting caught, fear of prison, or any form of retaliation.

Few knew that Hawke, originally William Wentworth Heuser, had an IQ in the genius category. While he read voraciously and with lightening speed, Hawke eschewed formal education. An inheritance from his parents allowed him to live comfortably without concern for traditional forms of employment and also permitted the isolation he demanded—even during his brief time on prison.

While the nickname, Hawke, derived from tormenting children who laughed at his beaklike nose and beady, onyx eyes, he found the name suited him. Adding an "e" to the end, Hawke use the name with the exclusion of legal documents. Most who knew him were not even aware of his given name. He preferred it that way.

When the phone rang, he knew it was Deirdre Warren. He wished he didn't need to keep the phone at all, but he was still tethered to that damned probation office. If not for that, he would have ripped the useless object out of the wall.

He knew he needed to talk to Dr. Warren, he just wasn't ready. He would call her—soon.

Hawke couldn't help but smile inwardly thinking about the frustration Jack must have felt when he didn't kill his former wife as intended. The truth was that he really did plan on killing the good doctor, but changed his mind. He owed Jack, after all, and usually paid his debts, but he never really liked the man.

Stiles would have been shocked to discover that Hawke's IQ exceeded his by nearly ten points. The little peacock loved to awe the other inmates with his twenty-dollar words, but never knew that Hawke understood all of them, probably better than he. Hawke intentionally used poor grammar as a way to confuse people like Jack. Let him think he was ignorant; it definitely worked to his advantage.

There was something about Deirdre Warren that appealed to Hawke. Not in a romantic or sexual way, but in a deeply human way. He didn't like people as a rule. In fact, he didn't know anyone he had ever liked. But he liked Dr. Warren. There was something genuine about her—and a little bit fragile.

It would have been very easy to snap her neck—as planned. When she smiled at him, without any guile or judgment, and offered him tea, he felt a caring he'd never experienced. They sat, him drinking his tea, her with her stupid mug of coffee, and chatted about life and prison and everything for over two hours. When she offered him the book he'd requested for Jack, he said to forget it. That's when he told her that he'd actually come to kill her—but changed his mind. Even then, Dr. Warren didn't seem to fear him. She seemed startled at his confession, but not afraid.

As a child, even his parents were afraid of him, and most of his classmates thought him a source of ridicule. He wore his inky black hair slicked back emphasizing the hawklike nose, which made them all titter. That is, however, until he killed one of them.

Ricky had been one of the group of annoying kids who constantly taunted Hawke, calling him *Hawkface, Hawkface*. When Hawke's favorite pocketknife went missing from his locker, he knew Ricky had taken it. The boy always watched when Hawke opened his locker. It had to be him.

Following him home from school, Hawke waited as, one by one, the others veered off, leaving Ricky alone. Silent and fast, Hawke came up behind him, raised the rock he had been carrying, and *bam*. It only took one hard slam od the rock to bring the boy down. Hawke stood over him for a minute, watching in curiosity as the blood seeped from Ricky's skull. Then, he deftly slip the pocketknife out of the boy's jacket and walked away. After that, he kept the knife with him always.

Since that first encounter, Hawke and Deirdre Warren had formed the closest thing to a friendship that he had ever experienced. He needed to let her know about Jack, but he had some information to gather first.

DEIRDRE

The phone rang unanswered, six, seven rings before Deirdre finally dropped the phone in frustration. Hawke refused to use an answering machine, and often just didn't pick up the phone if he didn't feel like it. The only reason he even agreed to a phone was that his probation officer insisted that he stay in contact. Nevertheless, Deirdre felt an intense urgency to talk to Hawke. Hawke was the one person who would tell her the truth, regardless of how much it would hurt her.

To say that Deirdre trusted Hawke was a gross exaggeration. True, he could have killed her and instead spared her life. True again she could have turned him in, but chose not to. The latter was a decision she questioned repeatedly. With his history, she wouldn't have any trouble convincing the police that she was telling the truth. Yet something stopped her. As much as she hated to admit it, Deirdre liked Hawke.

They often went for weeks, sometimes months, without speaking then he would call or show up just to say hello. Hawke was a man of very few words. Mostly, he would just nod, walk up the stairs, and sit waiting for the tea she ultimately handed him. Hawke never drank coffee, and even though it was her preference, Deirdre instinctively offered him tea instead. It was an instinct that may have actually saved her life.

She would talk; he would occasionally grunt or nod. On very rare occasions, he would say something so profound that she was floored by his insight. Then he would abruptly stand and leave without saying good-bye. Very strange man. But when Deirdre was troubled, she wanted to talk to Hawke.

She'd barely hung up the phone when it rang again.

"You wanted me?

"Not answering your phone again?" A grunt from Hawke.

"You know?"

"Yeah, he got out yesterday."

"So soon? I thought it might be a few months. Should I be worried?"

"He has some friends. Bad news guys. Some of them will do anything for him, kind of like cult worshippers. Stupid people think he's some kind of god. Just don't let anyone in you don't know. Don't call me for awhile. I'll be in touch."

"But..." The phone disconnected, and Deirdre listened to the dial tone. She groaned. Better warn her colleagues.

DEIRDRE

One of the things Deirdre liked best about the three colleagues with which she shared an office suite was that they hadn't been around during all the publicity about Jack. Sure, they knew her story. Who didn't? But they really didn't know Jack, and she needed to warn them that he might come to the office. They had no receptionist in the tiny waiting room, and anyone could enter from the parking lot.

The waiting room had only a small love seat and two chairs. A standing lamp and a small table covered with books and magazines completed the decor. They decided that they didn't need a larger room since they all prided themselves on never keeping their clients waiting.

It was an unwritten rule for all of them as they had all experienced the long, frustrating wait for professionals. They never wanted their clients to feel that form of frustration. Consequently, the room was used only if a client arrived early for an appointment.

Deirdre found an old photo of Jack, made copies for all three of them, and explained the situation. Her two male colleagues just nodded and assured her that they would let her know if anyone resembling Jack came around.

Rosie was another story. Just under five feet tall, Rosie was a dark Italian dynamo, who had also struggled with a painful divorce. She knew more of the story than the others since she and Deirdre had bonded over the past year.

"If that creep comes anywhere near this place, he'll wish he'd never been born. Don't worry, Hon, we'll watch your back."

Deirdre had to laugh at the mental image of Rosie confronting Jack.

"Hopefully it won't come to that, but I wanted you to know what he looked like, just in case. And, Rose, thanks."

Rosie winked and walked into her office.

Deirdre sat in her soft-brown leather chair, next to the large picture window, gazing out at the woods below. Her office was painted soft, warm beige, and colorful posters lined the walls along with her credentials in big mahogany frames. Two large comfortable chairs and a plush brown love seat completed the furnishings, along with a multicolored throw rug. It was a welcoming place, a shelter from the world.

Everyone loved being able to view the woods outside her window. They all said it was calming. Deirdre enjoyed those woods so much that she hadn't bothered to put up curtains or shades. Today, however, the woods looked different, more menacing. The small office complex had a large parking lot in the front of the building, and a smaller one behind it, connecting to the woods. On a busy day, they would have to park in the back, a fact that never bothered Deirdre—until today. Today she looked at her little silver Prius tucked in next to the back of the building and hoped that she could get out of there before dark. Shaking off the ominous cloud of fear, she went out to the waiting area to greet her first client of the day.

Deirdre's clients were a mixture of people with gambling problems, depression, anxiety, and some relational conflicts. All of them were intensely interesting to her. She was fiercely protective and devoted to their care, swearing to herself daily that she would never let anyone hurt them the way that Jack had the others.

Focusing on their unique issues was all consuming, and the bright day began to fade to dusk before Deirdre had time to think again about Jack. As the last client left her office, she realized that all the others had gone for the day and she would need to lock up.

Turning off each light, she moved from room to room, finally exiting into the waiting area. The group agreed to lock the door leading from the waiting room to the offices when there was only one therapist left. Today, Deirdre was relieved that someone had done that. Leaving the security of that locked door left her a bit uneasy, however.

As she locked the outside door, the parking lot was comfortably lighted and she could see lights from the passing cars; however, the back of the building was dim. The lights were always burning out or getting shot out by kids with BB guns. The lights that remained had a tendency to flicker and, sometimes, to go out entirely. They repeatedly had asked the landlord to fix them, but nothing had yet been done.

Moving briskly to her car she felt a silence coming from the woods. The quiet was usually soothing, but today it was threatening. She could disappear into those woods, she thought, and never be found. As she unlocked her car, she heard the distinct sound of movement behind her. Whirling around, she saw nothing.

"Imagining things, are we now?" She asked herself.

Nevertheless, she scooted into the car and quickly locked her doors, starting her engine with a sigh of relief. She couldn't go through this every evening. Hopefully, she could park in front tomorrow. Now she was eager to meet her friend, Karol, for dinner.

KAROL

Walking into the small dim restaurant, Karol scanned the room for her friend, Deirdre. She smiled at the prospect of spending a quiet evening with her longtime friend. Slipping onto a stool at the bar, she ordered a glass of chardonnay to sip while she waited. Karol shrugged off her coat, ran her hands through the long blonde hair, which had recently become streaked with gray, and took a deep breath. It had been a long day.

Ten years ago, Karol or Deirdre wouldn't have dreamed of sitting alone at a bar, even one attached to a restaurant. One of the few pleasures of aging, however, was that women of a certain age became invisible. While she received a few admiring glances, no one stared at her, considered hitting on her, or even noticed her presence, except the bartender.

Contrary to public opinion, older women alone tipped better than younger women alone, families, couples, or even men alone. At this time in their lives, they wanted the respect and convenience of good service and were willing to pay to get it. The bartender at this restaurant knew Karol and gave her that service eagerly. She didn't need to wait long, however, before her friend joined her, and they moved to a quiet table.

"I think I'm losing it," Deirdre confessed with an embarrassed laugh. "I actually thought someone was following me in the parking lot tonight. How silly."

Karol didn't share her friend's laughter. "I don't know if it's silly, Dee. You know what he's capable of. He's probably furious that Hawke never did the job. Who knows what other creeps he's encountered in the past few years."

"I guess you're right, but I just can't live in terror. I have to live my life."

"Well, you have Mike now."

Deirdre looked down at the diamond on her left hand and smiled. "Yes, I have Mike. But I don't want him to get caught up in this. The whole thing just seems so tawdry. It embarrassed me to have to tell him about it."

"Dee, you didn't do anything wrong. You just trusted the wrong man." Karol straightened and took a deep breath. "There's something I want to ask you to think about. Please don't say no right away."

"Is this about the gun thing again?"

"I don't think it would be a bad idea if you had one. I talked to my friend, and he said you could get a permit. I know how you feel about guns, Dee, but you need to be able to protect yourself."

Deirdre sighed. "You mean well, Karol, but I don't think I could use a gun on another human being, even Jack."

"Just think about it. Okay?"

"I'll think about it. Perhaps I could just go to one of those gun clubs and learn to use it. Oh, I don't know. The thought of it just makes me feel queasy. I do think I might take a self-defense class, though."

"Well, that's a start."

They both laughed. "Let's get another glass of wine," they both said in unison.

When Deirdre walked out of the restaurant, Karol sat for nearly an hour sipping the last of her chardonnay. She worried about her friend. Jack Stiles had nearly ruined Dee's life, and Karol felt somehow responsible for not stopping him. She couldn't help remembering the night she tried to convince Deirdre to walk away from him.

Deirdre had agreed that Jack was trouble and said she was going to end the relationship. Karol was dubious and insisted on going with her.

Deirdre appeared very strong and confident, but Karol was one of the few who knew how destroyed she had been when her twenty-year marriage ended suddenly in divorce. Her friend was emotionally fragile and an easy target for men like Jack Stiles. She had to get her away from him.

The minute Jack started talking to Deirdre in that low, whispery voice of his, Karol realized he had Deirdre mesmerized. There was nothing she could do to stop it. She just turned and walked away, leaving them together. So many times Karol wondered what would have happened if she'd stayed and tried to reason with her friend. She shook her head sadly. The only thing she could do now is keep her safe. Dee must realize how dangerous Jack Stiles could be. She had to protect herself. Karol would insist on it.

DEIRDRE

Being with her friend had lifted Deirdre's spirits. Karol was one of those friends you knew you could count on. They'd worked together for a while, making a powerful team. They were very different in many ways. Karol was all business, while Deirdre was about people and feelings. They seem to complement each other, and each respected the other profoundly. They remained friends even after they changed jobs and went their separate ways.

Deirdre sang along with the radio all the way home. Everything was going to be okay.

When she walked into her house, the phone was ringing. Still in her mellow mood, Deirdre lifted the phone. "Dr. Warren, may I help you?"

This time there was clearly breathing on the other line. The panic returning, Deirdre began to shout into the phone.

"Jack, is that you? What do you want from me? Leave me alone!"

She slammed the phone down, her mellowness changing to anger and frustration.

The phone rang again, almost immediately. "Jack, I told you, don't call me again."

"Dee Dee?"

Deirdre slumped into a chair. "Oh, Mike, I'm sorry, I..."

"What's going on? Why did you think I was Jack?"

"Oh, it's nothing. I'm just having one of my silly paranoid moments. How is your trip going?"

"Fine. Dee, is Jack out?"

"Mike, I...well, yes he is. It's just that I've been getting these calls. It's probably not even him."

"I'll cut my trip short and come home tomorrow."

"Don't you dare. I have my new alarm system. Jack wouldn't risk anything that would send him back to prison. If I see him anywhere near me, I can get a restraining order."

"You haven't seen him then?"

"No, I just found out that he was out. I guess I've been a little jumpy since then. I'm fine. I had a great dinner with Karol, a couple of glasses of wine, and now I'm going to go to bed and read for an hour. I'll see you at the end of the week. Don't worry."

"I don't know, Dee Dee, from what I've heard, he can be very lethal."

They chatted for a few more minutes as Deirdre assured him she was okay, murmured words of love, and said good night.

MIKE

Mike Bartlett was an extremely practical man. He wasn't given to unnecessary fears or fantasies, but he had heard in bits and pieces about Deirdre's ex. He even read her book—which was probably the only nontechnical book he had read since college. Jack Stiles reminded him a bit of his ex-wife, Joan. Joan was hysterical and demanding. He'd never thought of her as malevolent, however. Jack, on the other hand, appeared to be dangerous. He might cut this trip short, after all.

When Mike met Deirdre Warren, he had been licking his wounds from a nasty divorce. His wife had left him for another man, only to be dumped two months later.

She'd actually tried to resume the marriage following her dissolved affair, but Mike had drawn the line at infidelity and initiated divorce proceedings. He agreed to all her financial demands; he just wanted it to end.

He hadn't dated anyone since the divorce and had thrown himself into his business. Mike's social activities were limited to his weekly dinner with his daughter, Emily. She was the one bright spot in his life. He carried her picture with him on the road and called her daily to get the latest update on her life.

Even at twenty-eight, Emily was his little girl. From the moment she was born, there had been that connection, often to the exclusion of her mother. Joan had treated Emily with a coldness that Mike could never understand. It bordered on jealousy. In spite of Joan's indifference, or possibly because of it, Mike and Emily had bonded. It was Mike who rose in the early hours to rock and feed his daughter, and it was Mike who went to all her school plays and teacher conferences. Joan provided guidance on manners, clothes, and the selection of schools and friends. But it was Mike that Emily laughed and played with.

It was with Mike that Emily shared her secrets and her deepest wishes. He was hers, and she was his. Following the divorce, that bond became even tighter. Mike was concerned that Emily might resent Deirdre, but so far the two women seemed to have developed a genuine camaraderie.

Mike had no interest in dating and was more than reluctant to attend the dinner party where he'd met Deirdre Warren. His brother, Garvey, had recently fallen in love with a woman he'd only known a few weeks. He seemed to believe that everyone should be equally happy, particularly his older brother.

"I'm glad you found someone, Gar," he'd told his brother, "but that part of my life is over."

"Nonsense. You're only three years older than I am. We've both had bad marriages and been alone far too long. It doesn't have to stay that way."

"I'll go, but I'm telling you nothing is going to come out of this."

When he discovered that Deirdre Warren was in fact, Dr. Warren, he was convinced more than ever of the futility of this meeting.

"What am I going to talk to her about? I know nothing about psychology. I never even finished college. This is ridiculous."

DEIRDRE

Speaking with Mike always calmed Deirdre. She'd never dreamt she would finally meet the love of her life in her fifties. Jack had charmed her with his pseudo intellect and pretense of concern over world events. By the time she'd realized he was a fraud, it had been much too late.

Mike Bartlett was Jack's exact opposite. He was calm and unassuming, a big bear of a man with silver hair, bright blue eyes, and a warm smile. He had built a business after two years in college, dropping out to marry the woman who became the mother of his only child, Emily, now twenty-eight, and clearly the love of his life. Deirdre made a concerted effort not to interfere with their relationship.

Just one year ago, Deirdre reluctantly agreed to attend a dinner party with an old friend who had met a man through the internet. Kathy was clearly in love and wanted everyone to share the feeling. Deirdre was certain that love was not to be in her picture, but agreed to go to dinner and meet her friend's brother. When Deirdre entered Kathy's house, she could tell immediately that Mike Bartlett would rather be eating barbed wire than attending this dinner party. Deirdre shared his discomfort.

When she helped Kathy clear the table, she couldn't help overhearing Mike arguing with his brother. "A psychotherapist? What on earth would I have to say to her? You know I never even finished college."

Over coffee and dessert, Kathy and Mike's brother, Garvey, tried to incorporate Mike and Deirdre into the conversation. It became rapidly clear that they had nothing in common. Their politics were diametrically opposed, as was their choice in movies and reading material. Mike was a steak-and potatoes man and hated wine of any form. Deirdre wasn't much of a cook, but loved gourmet food and good wine. They finally agreed on football, both loved the Eagles.

As the evening wore on, however, she found herself laughing with Mike over some of the experiences related to his work and travel. Both of them hated business travel, the bad air in flight, horrible food in airports, and the austere hotel rooms. As reserved as he was, she found he had a great sense of humor. His laughter wasn't loud or raucous, but a deep, warm rumble.

In spite of their differences, Deirdre had begun to feel comfortable with Mike. When he smiled, that slow, easy grin, she felt warm and safe. Leaving together, he walked her to her car. She surprised herself by saying that she'd had a good time and he could call her if he liked. She handed him her card with the phone number.

Mike stuck the card in his pocket without glancing at the number, said a quick good night and moved toward his car.

Deirdre felt stung and convinced that she would never hear from Mike Bartlett again. It was actually two weeks later that he called. At first she wasn't sure who it was; his voice sounded garbled.

"I'm on my way to the airport," he shouted. Reception terrible. Wisconsin. Getting back late tonight. Dinner tomorrow?"

"Did you ask me to have dinner with you tomorrow?"

"Yes, dinner. Seven." The line disconnected.

Deirdre was shocked, but pleased. She had a date.

At exactly seven the next evening, Mike arrived at her door dressed in khakis and a dress shirt, open at the neck. It was the same outfit he had worn to dinner with Kathy and his brother. Deirdre would soon learn that was what he always wore, donning a suit and tie only when absolutely necessary. For some reason, that appealed to her. Jack had always spent a fortune of her money on designer suits and carried an expensive leather briefcase with nothing in it. Jack was all into image. Mike had no concern at all how he looked to others.

Mike dressed for convenience. His company contacts accepted his attire without issue. He was all business. They knew his word was good and his product, electrical supplies, quality. For Deirdre, Mike was like a safe warm cabin in the midst of a blizzard.

He grinned at her when she opened the door and she realized she was way overdressed.

"I'll go change."

"No, you look great. I should have brought flowers or something, but I'm not very good at that stuff."

"It's okay. Where are we going?"

"Steak house."

"Of course."

They both laughed.

Amazingly, they talked during dinner. While their lifestyles were different, they both shared the same basic values. They believed in honesty and trust and valued family. Deirdre's parents were both gone, but Mike had a wonderful mother whom he adored. She was clearly responsible for the man he was today.

The first time she met Mike's mother, she was terrified, but the small gray-haired, blue-eyed woman engulfed her in love. She was not only warm and caring, but extremely bright and witty, keeping up with politics and reading voraciously. She loved the Phillies with a passion and could tell you the batting averages of all players. This woman was clearly a dream and had raised two fantastic sons alone when their father died suddenly at a young age. Mike traveled a great deal for his business, so they saw each other sporadically. Nevertheless, he began calling her each night as an end to the day. The conversations were short, but she began to look forward to them.

"Plane ride was a nightmare. The woman in the seat next to me spent the entire flight consuming a huge Hoagie filled with onions. I think my clothes still reek. Needed to shower as soon as I hit the hotel."

Deirdre chuckled at the image of Mike suffering through the flight, knowing he would never say anything offensive to the woman. She would share some of her interesting moments, although she was limited due to confidentiality. Nevertheless, it was a good way to end the day.

Both a bit gun-shy about relationships, the first few dates neither made a move to touch, hug, or even shake hands. After about two months, as he left her house, he made an abrupt turn and kissed her quickly. He stood back and grinned, then walked away. She stood watching him, smiling.

Soon after the spontaneous kiss, Deirdre found herself curled next to him as they watched a movie that neither was really seeing. She looked up into those blue eyes and ran her fingers over his face, feeling the slight smoothness of his recent shave and smelling the faint scent of an old aftershave she remembered from long ago.

"Where have you been the past few weeks?" he grinned.

"Waiting for you," she sighed. "Right here waiting for you."

The kiss was slow this time and several hours later, they found themselves in the same place, still kissing.

"I guess I'd better go," he groaned. "This time."

The promise was very clear.

When they finally became intimate, it was so natural it seemed as though they had been together forever. It wasn't the frantic passion of the young, but a deep, fluid joining of two souls. Why had she had to wait so long for such intimacy?

Mike never stayed at her house, however. He always left before dawn. Mike Bartlett was a traditional man, he respected her reputation, and she loved him for it.

One Saturday morning, he surprised her by calling to ask if they could go shopping and then to lunch. She agreed readily, putting aside the paperwork she had planned for the day. Both usually caught up on work on Saturdays, getting together later in the day or evening. She assumed he needed her advice on clothes or household items.

Deirdre didn't ask where they were going shopping. She'd learned that Mike would tell her when he felt she needed to know. He didn't like wasting words. When they walked into the mall, she assumed they were headed for the men's store. Instead, he steered her into a jewelry store, heading directly toward the diamond rings.

"I didn't know what you would like, so I thought you could pick it out yourself."

She stared at him, mute.

"You want to get married, right?'

Deirdre began to laugh. "That was probably the most unromantic proposal any woman has ever had."

She pointed to a ring in the center of the glass. "I like that one."

Taking it from the case, the salesperson handed it to her. The ring slipped on her hand perfectly, as though it belonged there.

"Do you want mt to polish that for you?"

"No, I'm never taking it off." She looked up at Mike and smiled. He had his answer.

DEIRDRE AND EMILY

Deirdre's thoughts of Mike Bartlett always moved her to pick up his picture, which she kept in a prominent position on her desk. She talked to the picture when he was away. Somehow, it seemed to give her comfort. Her eye wandered to a nearby photo of a young blonde woman, Emily. The mouth was smiling, but the eyes were clouded.

Emily inherited Mike's bright blue eyes. Unlike her father, however, Emily's eyes didn't crinkle with laughter. They always seemed sad. Deirdre often wondered what kind of pain Emily carried around with her. The young woman was always smiling and affectionate with Mike. She clearly adored her father.

Deirdre was apprehensive about meeting Emily, concerned that she might resent sharing her father with a new woman who wasn't her mother; however, Emily was more than accepting. She behaved as though Deirdre has been in her life forever. Deirdre had actually asked her to be the maid of honor at the wedding, and Emily was so touched she had to leave the room.

Wanting to develop a friendship with Emily, Deirdre arranged a weekly luncheon so that they could get to know each other better. It was at one of these meetings that Deirdre noticed scars on the younger woman's arms.

Emily always wore long sleeves, even during hot weather. Respecting her privacy, Deirdre never asked her about her choice, but thought about it. As she reached for the salt, one afternoon, Emily's sleeve rode up her arm slightly, and Deirdre noticed the faint scars. During later outings, she couldn't help but notice that both arms were similarly marked. She asked Mike about it one evening when they were alone.

Mike hesitated for several long moments before responding. He'd never talked about Emily's issues with anyone, except her therapist. Nevertheless, he trusted Deirdre and knew her intentions were more than gossip or curiosity.

"Emily has had problems. She went to a therapist for a while and was taking some medication. She took the divorce very hard."

"So the problems were since the divorce?"

"Well, no. Actually, they started when she was twelve." He shook his head. "I never really understood what was wrong. She and her mother didn't seem to agree on much of anything, and I admit that I was away a lot." Mike shook his head as though to clear away the memories.

"She's fine now though. I think she really liked you."

Deirdre wanted to broach the subject with Emily, but didn't feel their relationship was close enough yet. Perhaps later. She couldn't help but worry about her prospective new stepdaughter, however. There was an ongoing melancholy about the young woman.

It was difficult not to compare Mike, his daughter, and Emily's mother. All three had the same blue eyes. Mike's were warm, Emily's sad, but Joan's eyes were icy and cold. Both women were strikingly beautiful, but Joan's facial structures held years of anger and resentment, giving her a hard, angular look. Even her voice was tinged with an edge, as though she were gritting her teeth while talking.

Joan clearly resented Emily and even attempted to convince Mike that the marriage would be a mistake. Mike told Deirdre that Joan worried about Emily's inheritance.

"But you've taken care of her future. Emily will be fine."

"I've told both of them that. Emily says she doesn't care, but Joan won't let it go. Hey, let's not let Joan dampen our happiness, Dee. She has nothing to do with me anymore."

Deirdre had smiled and agreed, but couldn't help but wonder what effect Joan's hostility had on her daughter. Perhaps this new man in Emily's life would turn all of that around. She wouldn't tell them his name, only that she had met someone new, and he was special. Emily's smile was so genuine, that Deirdre couldn't help but be happy for her. She only hoped this man would not hurt her. Emily had experienced enough hurt a lot in her life.

Someday, in the future, Deirdre planned to have a long talk with Emily about her past. Maybe, just maybe, she could help her.

EMILY

Emily Bartlett had a secret life. She loved to prowl the bars down in the city, an area of which her family would never approve. Sometimes she met guys. Sometimes she went home with them. Mostly, though, she just flirted and had fun. She knew it was risky to have unprotected sex, especially with guys she met in these places, but the risk made her feel better. Taking risks relieved the tension, like the cutting.

She'd had to stop the cutting though, because it caused too much concern for her parents. They'd make her go back to that shrink if she kept it up. She'd hated that doctor. He kept calling her *borderline* and talking about boundaries. Nothing like her new doctor. Dr. Wakefield understood her. He was special and very secret. They didn't need to know about him or her nightly prowls.

No one at the bank where she worked would see her here. None of them would be caught dead in this neighborhood. Emily never expected to meet *him* in a place like this, but here he was and, boy, was she hooked.

The first time she met Scotty, she had been sitting right here at this very stool at the end of the bar. She smiled, remembering, while she waited for him to arrive.

"I know you've heard this many times before, but you are the most beautiful woman in this place."

"I'm the only woman in this place, except the bartender."

She'd looked up at him, intending to tell him to get lost, taken one look into those turquoise eyes, and felt her whole body turn to warm honey. Her smile was all the invitation he needed.

"I think you have saved my life," he whispered, taking her hand. "I never expected to find an angel in the pit of hell, but here you are."

Emily laughed, but she also blushed deeply and felt a tingling inside that removed any last bit of resolve she might have had.

"So why are you here in this pit of hell? Mister?

"Oh, just call me Scott. I have been so involved in my medical research that I haven't talked to a human being in ages. I took an apartment nearby. Yes, I know it is a terrible neighborhood, but I needed privacy. As a physician, I am often recognized by former patients. I wanted quiet and also must have yearned for something I didn't even know existed until I met you." He began stroking the palm of her hand very gently.

"So now tell me about you? What is an angel doing here?" He looked around in disgust.

"Well, the truth is I live on the other side of town, but come here also not to be recognized."

"Kindred souls," he whispered and began quoting a line from a poem she vaguely remembered from college.

The sound of his voice was like a potion. The words were irrelevant. She just wanted him to continue talking and stroking her palm.

"I need to hold you and touch you, my angel. I can't take you to my room. It is so barren, it would be offensive to your beauty."

Emily smiled, pulled out her car keys, and took his hand firmly in hers. "Come with me."

Later, Emily would learn that he was a widower; his wife had died from a rare disease three years before. Her death drove him to give up his surgical practice and go into research. He hadn't been with another woman since his wife's death, but he felt unexplainably drawn to Emily. She felt the same way. It was fate that brought them together. He was everything she had ever wanted. He was loyal. He wouldn't leave her the way her father had, the way all the men in her life had, just because she'd had some problems. Scott was her love.

SCOTT

He spotted her immediately. She was the one he'd been searching for. Head bent toward her glass, slumped posture as she leaned against the bar, she might as well have been telegraphing her loneliness. Vulnerability, though, that was what he'd recognized. She was ripe for him. He needed a fresh place to hide out, and he needed someone new to share his feelings. Well, at least the feelings that she would hear about.

Scott didn't need his usual strategies. Emily seemed to be waiting for him. She was his with the first corny line, "You are the most beautiful woman in this bar."

When she looked up at him, the pain in her eyes was palpable. He almost felt guilty for the way he would use her. Almost.

He bought her several drinks, just enough to make sure she wouldn't resist his final move. He stuck to club soda; alcohol numbed his excitement.

He gently stroked the palm of her hand, maintaining contact at all times. Staring into her eyes, he spoke in his whisper of a voice telling her how he had lost his wife and dedicated his life to medical research, giving up his medical practice. As she melted toward him, breath quickening with each touch, he finished her off.

"I know you will think me insane for saying this, but the moment I saw you my heart leapt. I knew you were the only woman I would ever want again. Let's leave this place and go where we can be alone. My place is far too cold for someone as warm ang alive as you." He looked down sadly. "After I lost my wife, I didn't care how I lived. Until now."

He looked up at her smiling.

What few things he had were in the trunk of his car. He moved them to Emily's that night. She was his.

CHAD

Dr. Chad Wakefield was in his glory. Sitting tall in the witness chair, he smiled as the entire courtroom hung on his every word.

As a forensic psychologist, Chad often gave expert testimony in court. Today was one of those days. He smoothed his expensive dove gray cashmere jacket and continued with his extensive list of credentials. Then without prompting from the defense attorney, Dr. Wakefield launched into a lengthy, very esoteric explanation of his client's state of mind, history, and reasons why this man was completely innocent of all charges.

Giving the jury the benefit of his most sincere look, he rose slowly from the witness stand. The jurors never took their eyes from him as he walked toward his seat. The silence that greeted him convinced Dr. Chad Wakefield that this would be an easy verdict of *not guilty*.

God, he loved this. It was power, pure and simple.

People were such sheep. Most of them were stupid and easily lead. He seldom encountered a real challenge, but occasionally, he met someone who challenged his ability. When this happened, he was like a wolf on a hunt, loving every moment, every twist and turn of the game.

Leaving the courtroom, he quickly checked his smartphone for messages. There were three from Emily. He would let her wait a while longer, making her more anxious and grateful for his call. She wasn't much of a challenge. Desperate for his approval, she would do anything he asked. He loved to toy with her and observe her pain and panic.

Chad loved the control he had over his patients. There was no career, even politics—although he had been approached lately about running for office—that allowed him that much complete power over others. The trust and dependence was intoxicating.

It was the second message on his voice mail that really picked his interest.

Jack Stiles.

What could he possibly want?

Chad had followed the Stiles case with interest. Too bad Jack hadn't contacted him earlier. Things might have turned out differently. It would be interesting to mentor someone with his potential.

Chad had met Jack's ex wife, Dr. Warren, at a couple of social events. Most of his colleagues were in awe of him, but Deirdre Warren had looked at him with disdain, almost as though she could see into his heart. It made Chad shiver a bit thinking about it. Most people didn't recognize his true identity. Too bad she hadn't been as astute with her ex-husband. He vowed to wipe that superior look off her face.

Chad Wakefield had been on the board when they took Deirdre Warren's license. Most of the members had wanted to give her a reprimand. She hadn't actually done anything wrong after all.

With satisfaction, he remembered how he had convinced them to revoke her license completely.

"It is our duty," he said, *"to protect society from such a menace." "She had,"* he said, *"allowed Jack Stiles to violate the trust of her clients."*

When he finished, he could have called for her execution. He chuckled with the memory.

He thoroughly enjoyed her misery and had hoped to reduce her to tears and hysterics before she left the hearing. As she walked away, however, she'd merely held his gaze for a long moment, kept her head up, and turned toward the door. He'd experienced a flicker of irritation. Tears would have been better.

He dialed the number Stiles had left. The game wasn't over yet. Perhaps he could bring the bitch to tears after all.

EMILY

Emily paced the floor, digging her nails into the scars along her arms left over from her years of cutting. Daddy had actually proposed to that witch. How could he could he do this to her?

Daddy had no idea how she really felt about Deirdre. She'd always smiled and pretended to be the bitch's friend. Deep down though, she knew it was just temporary. Daddy would see right through that woman's simpering act and come back to being hers exclusively. But it didn't seem to be working out that way. With each day Daddy and that woman were together, the panic kept building inside of her. Emily felt she might explode with anger and frustration.

Why wasn't Dr. Wakefield calling back? She had called hours ago. Didn't he know how upset she was?

After hearing the news about the engagement, Emily had run to the apartment hoping to see Scotty. He would help her, tell her what to do. He would understand.

The apartment was so quiet. The minute she entered the apartment, she knew he wasn't there. It was too silent. He always played classical music at top volume. He claimed it helped him concentrate. There was no music; no Scotty.

He must be at the library doing research. Why didn't he have a computer? Everyone did research on the Web.

He'd told her he preferred the medical library at Hopkins. It was worth the two-hour drive. Hopkins had the best medical library in the country according to Scotty. Sometimes he would be away for days, claiming he was too tired to drive home after working all day. Emily was never sure exactly what he was supposed to be researching, and he never appeared to do anything with all those hours at the Hopkins Library. But she knew he was a genius and whatever he did would be something incredible.

But she needed him with her now. She was getting more frantic with each moment. Finally, she heard his key in the lock and sighed with relief. Scotty was home at last. He would help her. He would tell her what to do.

CHAD

Chad gazed lovingly out the window from his tenth-floor loft. He loved the height and the vista spread out before him. The blinking light on his desk told him his next client was waiting, but that was fine. She could wait. The longer they waited, the more grateful they were to actually see him. By the time, he could get them to do just about anything he wanted.

No, not sex. He never had sex with his clients. Not because he considered it unethical, but because it just didn't appeal to him. He preferred other forms of power; sex was too short-lived. Perhaps, inflicting pain might be interesting, but no, too risky. This was much safer and much more stimulating.

He's actually tried sex frequently with both males and females before he decided to marry someone that would worship him and not be very demanding. His wife, Julie, was such woman. When she looked up at him with those big doggy brown eyes, he could have asked her to commit mass murder, and she would have done so eagerly, anything to please him.

Julie bored him completely, but took care of all the necessary annoyances that he had no desire to attend to. He gave her a nice home, two equally boring children, and had sex with her once or twice a month to keep her happy.

The fact that he never seemed interested in any of his attractive clients earned him the nickname Father Chad. Wakefield found that hysterical. Oh, yes, he went to church visibly every Sunday morning, sang loudly, and gave generously. He was also an elder. More power, of course. It was amazing how much trust was given to anyone who claimed to be a devout believer.

Unfortunately, there were always a few who somehow recognized him for what he was. Usually, he could neutralize them quickly. He'd nearly done so with Deirdre Warren, but somehow she'd managed to survive. Too bad!

He'd only seen Dr. Warren once since she regained her license. They were both at a retirement luncheon for a mutual colleague. He watched her from across the room, making sure she was alone before approaching her.

"Why, Dr. Warren, so happy to hear that you are back among the practicing professionals." He frowned sympathetically. *"So sorry about my role in your hearing, but after all, we need to protect our clients' welfare."*

She'd looked at him as though he were a piece of filthy gum on her shoe.

"Save it," she'd said quietly and walked away without another look.

God, he hated that woman.

Time to let Emily in. He had some interesting plans for her. Plans that involved Deirdre Warren. The thought made him smile broadly.

EMILY

Emily had always wanted to love her mother. More importantly, she'd wanted her mother to love her. Her mother had taught her manners, how to dress, wear makeup and get into the right schools. She'd never taught her how to love. Daddy was the one who did that.

When Daddy walked in the door, Emily always managed to be the first one to welcome him. She would launch herself into his arms before he could even close the door behind him. Often, they fell down laughing and hugging each other. Daddy was glad to see her. The smile died when Mommy walked in.

Somehow, Emily knew that Mommy hated their nightly rituals. The only time she could really enjoy being with her father was when her mother was out of the room, or even better, out of the house.

The cutting started when she turned thirteen. She'd begun to develop into a beautiful young woman. It seemed that the more developed Emily became, the less her mother loved her. She would make comments to Emily about being slutty, encouraging her to behave in a more ladylike manner in front of her father.

It isn't proper for a young woman to hang on her father like that. People might get the wrong impression. It's unnatural.

Emily wasn't really sure what her mother meant, but the message was clear that she was not to get too close to her father. When they divorced, Emily was blamed. Her mother was in a rage constantly when she was around. That was when the cutting began.

She tried desperately to calm her mother down and to please her. Nothing helped. The stress was so intense that she would cut her arms and legs at night. It was the only thing that relieved the tension.

Daddy was the first to notice the scars and blamed himself. He was beside himself with guilt and insisted that she see a psychiatrist. He was a horrible old man and seemed to blame her for everything. She agreed to stop cutting if she could stop seeing him.

Her parents agreed to send her to boarding school, and while Emily hated the school, it was better than having to deal with her mother. The best part was that Daddy drove up to have dinner with her every weekend. She finally had time alone with him. He promised her he would never leave her, that he would always be there for her.

She loved seeing her father on the weekend, but still felt the constant tension building. Cutting was out of the question, as she was checked regularly by the school nurse.

She had been given a cute sports car for her sixteenth birthday and began going out for drives late at night after bed check. That was when she discovered the other side of the world, the seedy bars and clubs, and people who couldn't care less where you went to school or who your parents are.

Sex with someone she's never met before or would see again was almost as good as the cutting—until it was over. Afterward, she'd drive home feeling empty. There was no time she could be happy was with her daddy.

DEIDRE

Deirdre was just about to turn off the lights and call it a night when the phone rang again. She considered letting the call go to voice mail, but could never let a phone ring unless she was with a client.

The voice on the other end was so faint; Deirdre almost thought it was another one of those calls. Then she heard the voice, a soft feminine voice that sounded distraught. "Dr. Warren?"

"Yes, how can I help you?"

"You were married to Jack Stiles?"

Deirdre was instantly on alert. "Who is this? Did Jack tell you to call me? Is he there?"

"No, no. Please don't hang up. He doesn't know I'm calling. He would be very upset if he knew I'd talked to you. I just. I need."

"What?"

"I don't know exactly. I just thought if I talked to you I might understand better. I'm so confused."

Deirdre sighed in understanding. She remembered the confusion, the frustration. This was another of Jack's victims.

"Tell me what's going on. First, what's your name?"

"Susan, Susan Carmichael. I own a house and rent out the third floor to tenants from time to time for extra money. My husband died." She didn't say anything for a few seconds, and then continued. "Jack rented the room. He'd been in prison, but he said it wasn't his fault, that he'd just been protecting you. I felt sorry for him. He seemed so sad."

Deirdre knew just how sad and helpless Jack could appear, and what effect it had on women who wanted to help him. Susan was obviously another one of those.

"Go on, Susan. So then what?"

"Well, he would make me dinner. He's really a good cook." She began to cry.

"Susan, what did he do?"

"He said he loved me, that he'd never loved anyone else since his first wife died, and that he'd never loved you."

"I understand. Has he taken any money from you?"

"Well, he wanted to go out and get the mail for me everyday. I thought that was sweet, but then I started to notice things were missing. I called the bank and they said that I'd opened a new credit card. I never did. I think Jack has been lying to me."

"Yes, I'm afraid he does that quite a lot. What else happened?"

"He said he needed money to send to his mother in Indiana. She's very sick. He said he'd start to pay it back when he got a job. He doesn't seem to be looking very hard for a job. I found his mother's number and called her, but she said she's fine and never got any money from him." Susan began crying harder.

"Susan, how much money did he get from you?"

"Ten thousand dollars."

"Has he given any of it back?"

"No, he keeps saying that when we're married what's mine is his anyway. I'm scared. I feel like such a fool."

"Susan, you need to tell Jack if he doesn't give you the money back you will contact his probation officer. That will put a scare into him."

"That's the problem, Dr. Warren."

"What?"

"He's gone. Jack is gone. The first night, I thought he was just mad because I had insisted he get a job, but then he didn't come home again. It's been a week. I called his probation officer, and he said that Jack never checked in for his weekly appointment. They have a capias out on him." The sobbing got stronger. Susan was gulping back her tears, her words getting more and more incoherent. "I am so stupid."

"No, Susan, you are not stupid, just trusting. You aren't the first woman he's duped, and you won't be the last. If he shows up, call the police. And Susan, most important, change all your accounts. He could clean you out if he has those numbers."

"Okay, I'll do that the first thing in the morning. Dr. Warren?"

"Yes?"

"Can I call you again?"

"Of course, Susan. Call me anytime. Good night."

"Thanks. Night."

Deirdre hung up the phone. She'd never be able to sleep tonight. What was Jack up to now? Why had he disappeared? He could have easily handled Susan. He's up to something. But what?

The first thing in the morning, she was on the phone to Jack's probation officer.

"Why can't you find him?" Deirdre yelled. "You're his probation officer."

"Dr. Warren, I put a capias out on him. That's all I can do. It's really out of my hands. When the police pick him up, we can violate him."

"What does that mean?"

"It means that when they pick him up, we will put him back in prison for violation of probation. That is, unless he has a good reason for disappearing."

"Until then?"

"Until then, the police will look for him. They are checking all his usual haunts. The trouble is, Jack Stiles doesn't have any friends other than ex-cons, and they aren't talking. We contacted his folks, but they haven't heard from him, and I doubt that he would have gone out there. Sorry, Dr. Warren, we're doing all we can."

Deirdre looked again at the sheet of paper crumpled in her fist. She had opened her front door this morning to retrieve the paper when she noticed an envelope stuck under the door knocker. The one sheet of paper held the words,

YOU WILL PAY

The words were cut out from newsprint and taped on the paper. She had immediately called the police, and they agreed to come and pick it up. They suggested she notify Jack's probation officer, but said they had no evidence that he had sent the note.

Deirdre knew, without a doubt, that the note was from Jack. The worst thing was that it wasn't mailed. He had been there, touched her door. She was so glad she had changed the locks years ago. Could he still get in? Her mind raced with questions. One thing she knew for certain: Jack Stiles had disappeared, and now he was going to get even with her for helping put him in prison nine years ago. This nightmare never seemed to end.

Frustrated, Deirdre hung up the phone. She knew Jack had managed to disappear from the police in the past. It was only when one of the women caught on to him and turned him in that they were able to find him. He could evade the authorities indefinitely. In the meantime, what was she supposed to do?

She listened to the dial tone for a few seconds and then punched in a familiar number. "Karol? What was the name of that gun club you recommended?"

DEIDRE

"*Krav Maga?* Karol, what in the world is that?"

"*Krave Maga* in Hebrew stands for hand-to-hand combat. It began in Israel in 1948 and was used by the Israeli Defense Forces. In the United States, it was picked up by the FBI and some of the police forces, including NYPD. The important thing for you to know is that it's one of the best self-defense techniques for women, quick and easy to learn and very effective. I found a *Krav Maga* training center just a few miles from your house."

"Wow, you've been doing your homework. What about the gun? I thought you were pushing for me to get a gun."

"I still think you should have one, just in case, and I have a list of gun shops that offer lessons. But I don't think you can rely on that alone. What if he sends someone like Hawke again, only this time you won't be so lucky. Suppose you turned your back, and he grabbed you, and..."

"Okay, okay, I get the picture. I still haven't decided for sure about the gun. You know how I feel about guns. I would probably end up shooting myself in the foot, or shooting the cat by mistake. I'm so jumpy. I'm not sure

I trust myself with anything so lethal. I like the idea of self-defense though. I'll call them today."

"Whew, I'm so relieved."

""You really think he's going to come after me, don't you?"

Karol didn't speak for a minute, but then agreed. "Yes, Dee, I do. I hear things. Someone told me that when he read your book about him, he was in a rage. He completely destroyed the cell. They had to send someone in to give him a shot of something. Dee, he hates you. I'm sorry, but you need to be careful."

"I know. I just never thought of him as dangerous—at least not physically. I always knew he couldn't be trusted with money, but I thought he was harmless. For a psychotherapist, I'm not such a good judge of character."

"Don't go there again, Dee. He fooled a lot of people. You were in love with him; you wanted him to be what he pretended."

"Um, hmm. I guess you're right. I still feel stupid though, for not seeing through him. Okay, I'll do the self-defense thing, and then I'll think about the gun. Happy?"

"Yes, but, Dee, don't wait too long."

KRAV MAGA

Deirdre wasn't sure exactly what to expect, but the tiny woman standing before her in a tight, black-knit exercise suit was not it. She had decided against a group class and opted for a single session alone— at least for now. The woman, whose name was Bridey, stood just about five feet tall and couldn't have weighed more than eighty pounds. Yet she seemed to have an energy that equaled five jumbo cups of espresso. She'd served in the Israeli Army, Deirdre discovered. *She must have amazing skills*, she thought.

Her hair stood in dark spikes on her head, and her gleaming black eyes appeared almost too large for her tiny head. Speaking in a voice that sounded as though she had a bad chest cold, Bridey asked what Deirdre wanted from the session.

"I may be in danger," Deirdre offered tentatively. "My friends think I need to be able to protect myself."

"Have you ever been attacked?"

"No, not really."

"You're never actually prepared for what happens. It comes at you suddenly, without warning. Stops your breath, confuses you. It is important that you act immediately and not allow yourself to be overwhelmed.

Most of all, never allow yourself to be taken away from a safety area."

"Safety area?"

"A place where you may potentially get help, a public place or close to the public. Once you are alone, in his car, or in the woods or any isolated area, you lose the advantage."

"Okay, so how do I stop that?"

"You need to use the wet cat."

"Wet cat? Did you say wet cat?"

"Yes. Did you ever try to hold a wet cat? It claws, it bites, it wiggles, it moves every muscle. You can't hold it, no matter how small it is. You, miss, must become a wet cat. Kick, claw, bite, do everything in your power to move away from your attacker so that you can use the moves I will show you today."

Deirdre smiled. A wet cat, huh? She liked that.

Bridey continued, "Understand that in *Krav Maga* our goal is to put our opponent out of commission as fast as possible and end the conflict. So we target the most vulnerable parts such as the eyes, jaw, throat, groin, and knee. We use the most efficient and effective tools, including the head if necessary, and of course, arms and legs."

Bridey began demonstrating punches such as the straight punch, palm heel strike, hammerfist, and some elbow strikes. She then showed Deirdre the leg techniques which included the front kick, round kick, side kick, back kick, and heel kick.

The tiny woman whirled and kicked and struck with such speed and force that Deirdre could barely follow her. But after each astonishing move, Bridey would stop and show the steps, which turned out to be quite simple. Using the fist as a hammer, keeping the thumb tucked in made sense. Striking the hammerfist to the bridge of the nose would be a quick and disabling move. The goal was to disable and get away, not to continue the conflict.

"You want to use what works the fastest depending on your position. Most important, you want to take your opponent by surprise. We want to stay off the ground as much as possible, but if put to the ground, use the ground kicks like this." Bridey demonstrated a few ground kicks and arm bars, something called the guillotine and triangle choke.

"If your wrists are pinned, use your legs or knees to loosen the hold. Remember, there are no rules in *Krav Maga*, just go for it with whatever you can use. And don't forget the wet cat."

Deirdre loved the wet cat, but realized she would need a few more sessions to learn all of the techniques Bridey had demonstrated.

All women need to learn this, she thought.

Upon leaving the first session, Deirdre turned and hugged her petite instructor. "Thank you. This gives me a little hope. I was feeling so helpless, and I hate that feeling."

Bridey merely nodded somberly. She knew her student was far from safe.

DEIRDRE

Deirdre felt sore everywhere. There wasn't a muscle that didn't scream when she moved. Who said this was easy? The worst thing was that she wasn't completely convinced she could use it. Her confidence from the training session had all but dissipated. All this talk about possible stalkers had put her on edge. She knew it had to be her imagination, but it seemed that she always felt a presence nearby, like a shadow.

Tonight she limped from her car following her latest lesson. At the front door, she hesitated, looking around. Did that bush move? Was it the wind? No, none of the trees were blowing. The night was still. Yes, she was certain that bush moved. As she quickly inserted her key in the lock, she felt a warm breeze against the back of her neck as though someone were breathing behind her.

She turned quickly, snapping her neck, but there was no one behind her. Slipping inside she turned the dead bolt and hit the hall light. She smiled at the sight of her cat, Pax, but noticed her fur was ruffled, her ears were back. Did she hear something, too?

Are we both losing it, Pax? She picked up the cat and stroked her fur until the familiar purring began. Then she noticed the envelope on the floor in front of the door.

Hands shaking, she tore open the envelope. It was the same newsprint letters. Only this time it read,

YOU WILL FEEL PAIN

At first she thought he'd been inside, but then she realized he had managed to slide it just under the front door. Another attempt to rattle her even more.

No!

She crumbled the note and threw it at the door.

I won't let you do this to me. I won't.

Deirdre sank to the floor crying in anger and fear. Pax watched her curiously and scrambled into the other room. A few minutes later, Deirdre stood and pulled the list of gun clubs from her purse. She would call tomorrow. She would not be his victim again.

THE GUN

Deirdre had always had an intense hatred of guns and supported gun control laws. However, she was getting more and more terrified and decided she needed to do whatever she could to protect herself.

After many hours of research, in total frustration, Deirdre called Karol to complain. "I have no idea what I'm looking for. I called five different gun shops and clubs, but how do I know which one is right for me? One guy sounded like we were preparing for another civil war. Another wanted me to join a survival group. Good grief, Karol, I don't think I can do this."

"Calm down. I will pick you up Sunday morning. It will be fine. Just leave it to me."

Sunday morning, right on time, Deirdre greeted her friend at the front door.

"Thank you for doing this, Karol, but I'm really not sure I can go through with it"

Ignoring her friend's doubts, Karol drove to a nearby gun club where she was greeted warmly by the owner and several members.

"You never told me you were a member of a gun club."

Karol laughed nervously. "Well, I know how antigun you are and saw no reason to get into it with you."

Karol set Deirdre up with goggles and a headset and pulled her into a chute with targets set up in front. She began to lay out a series of handguns and inserted cartridges into each one then fired a few rounds into the targets.

Before allowing Deirdre to touch the guns, Karol ran her through a brief training on how to load, use, and maintain the weapon.

"Most importantly," Karol cautioned unnecessarily, "never point a weapon at anyone unless you intend to use it. Even though you believe it is empty; always assume the gun is loaded." Karol then showed her how a bullet could still be in the chamber even though one thought it was empty.

Looking intently at her friend, Karol continued. "Dee, I know you hate guns, and many people use them for the wrong reasons. Many people do not respect them and avoid taking the proper training to learn how to use them safely. But others register their guns and take thorough training in how to use them. I don't doubt that you know which category I fall into."

Karol sighed and continued in a shaky voice. "When I was five, I woke suddenly in the middle of the night. I could hear my mother crying and some muffled noise. I was afraid, but curious, so I tiptoed into their room. My parents were both tied up, my father gagged. He kept making angry noises as two men in masks held my mother down. She was crying, and I could see they were hurting her. I wanted to rush at them and save my parents, but somehow I knew I couldn't help them. They never saw me. I crept back to my room and crawled deep into the back of my closet."

Deirdre gasped in shock and put her arms around her friend. "I had no idea. God, I am so sorry."

"I was in the closet for hours until my father came and found me. I could hear them calling my name, but was afraid to come out. The men had taken my mother's jewelry, including her wedding rings. They took some other stuff, but I don't remember. I only remember the rings because my mother was so distraught. It was many years later that I understood that both men had raped her while my father was forced to watch. Afterward, my father bought a gun. We all learned out to use it and were instructed on safety issues. Then they put the gun in a safe place only taking it out monthly for target practice. We vowed never to be victims again."

"All the time we've known each other, shared so much together, and you never told me about this."

"I don't really like to talk about it. I just wanted you to know that I had a reason to get involved with guns. I take lessons and practice at least once a month. I am licensed to carry, and I always have a gun with me. Deirdre, I am not just some nutcase who wants to exercise power, and I don't kill Bambi. I just want to feel some level of control. Now, it is time to get started." The discussion was over.

People were shooting targets on either side of them, and Deirdre began to feel panic rising in her chest. Even with the ear protection, each shot from neighboring chutes sent an electric jolt through her. Did she really want to do this?

Karol turned toward her and handed her a small black revolver. "This is the easiest to shoot and has the least kick." "Kick? What do you mean, kick?"

Karol nodded at the shells on the floor beside them and in the neighboring chutes. "The shells kick back at you sometimes. That's why you need the goggles. Don't worry, it doesn't hurt. Here, take the gun."

Deirdre reached her hand toward the black object in Karol's hand. It seemed to transform itself into a coiled, black snake. She pulled her hand back as though it had bitten her.

"Come on, Dee, you can do it. It's easy."

Shaking her head and feeling sure she would vomit any second, Deirdre ripped off the goggles and earmuffs.

"I'll wait outside."

Minutes later, Karol found her friend gulping deep breaths and shaking outside the car.

"Karol, I'm so sorry. You went to all this trouble. I feel like such a wimp, but I just couldn't do it. I could not use that *thing* on any living being. I just can't."

"Hey, don't worry. It takes some getting used to." She handed Deirdre a package. Don't open it now. We can talk about it over a glass of wine—or two."

Sitting in the comfort of her living room, Deirdre sipped her wine and reluctantly opened the box her friend had given her.

"I know, Dee, just keep it. I will give you more instructions ono how to load it later, and we can talk about it. You can keep it locked up, and you never have to use it. I will feel better just knowing you have it."

"Deirdre handed her friend a small key. "Put it in the safe at the top of the closet and lock it up. I don't want to look at it right now."

Karol nodded solemnly and did as her friend requested.

One step at a time, she thought.

Hopefully, Deirdre would be able to use it if she needed to. Something told her that time might come soon.

Deirdre thanked her friend, said good night, and then sat, deep in thought, for over an hour. Perhaps it was a good time to talk to Tina.

TINA

Tina Angelina-Smith was a dark beauty closely resembling Demi Moore. In spite of her looks, though, she was anything but glamorous. She had been born Antoinette Marie Angelina into a traditional Italian, Catholic family. If she'd been a boy, she would have been directed into the priesthood. As a female, however, becoming a psychologist was the next best thing—unless, of course, she agreed to the convent. Tina, as she preferred to be called, wanted desperately to please her family, but adamantly refused the convent. They agreed to a good Catholic college and made her promise to always help people. She agreed.

Her family suspended all contact with her when she blatantly gave up her practice in shame after marrying John Smith. Unlike Deirdre, Tina made no effort to recapture her professional reputation. She had made the unforgivable mistake of falling in love with a client.

John Smith had never actually been Tina's client; however, he was the husband of her client. Tina's client, which she'd quickly diagnosed as a borderline personality disorder, spent her therapy sessions complaining about her husband, John. He was inconsiderate, never home, didn't appreciate her. The litany continued week after week.

According to John's wife, it was his fault that she repeatedly sought out high-risk behaviors. She had frequent affairs with dangerous men, once contracting a venereal disease. She ran up credit card debt and gambled on high stakes slots several times a week.

Tina never wanted to ignore a complaint of abuse, regardless of the circumstances. So after obtaining a release from his wife, she decided to attempt to see Mr. Smith herself. Surprisingly, he agreed immediately, seeming almost relieved at the request.

When John Smith walked into her office, Tina was immediately staggered by the look of pain on his face. He looked beaten down both emotionally and physically. There were unhealed scratches on his face, and he seemed embarrassed.

"In the beginning, she was so grateful for my help," he began. She said I'd saved her from an abusive life. I felt like her shining knight and wanted to do anything I could for her. Perhaps if we could have had children? After the first miscarriage, she began to complain that I wasn't there for her, that I didn't Understand her needs.

"I tried everything I could to make her happy. I needed to work more hours. As a chemical engineer, I make good money, but she liked nice things and kept opening credit cards. I wanted to talk to her about them. That was the first time she got violent. She started screaming and throwing things. When I tried to calm her down, she scratched me. Then she called the police and said I hit her. They could see that I was the one with the marks and threatened to charge her. I asked them not to and agreed to get her some help."

At this point in time, John put his head in his hands and wept. Tina had never felt so helpless in her life, and so sorry for another human being. Tina had never been able to guard her emotions at work and often radiated the pain she felt for her clients. She knew it was a weakness as a therapist but was unable to stop the intense empathy.

The sessions with John and his wife, Laura, continued for months. Sometimes Tina felt she was making headway, and then there would be another incident. In spite of the psychiatric recommendations to the contrary, Laura managed to get Xanax from a physician and took an overdose that she swore was accidental. Laura was hospitalized for a week, but then missed her next appointment with Tina.

Tina called to reschedule and finally got John on the phone. He sounded exhausted and very depressed.

"I don't know where she is. She packed a bag and left the day after she was released. I have called everyone and even filed a missing person report. The police will probably be contacting you soon."

Two days later, John Smith called Tina and requested a meeting out of her office. She explained that was not her routine, but he sounded so desperate, that she finally agreed. He was not her client, but Tina still felt uncomfortable about it. Yet she couldn't ignore his desperation.

When John entered the coffee shop, the man Tina greeted was a completely different human being. His eyes were clear, his step smart, and when he took her hand, it was though an electric shock went through them both.

"Tina, I know this is unusual, but I had to talk to you away from your office."

Tina ignored the fact that he was using her first name, as he had always referred to her as Dr. Angelino. She merely nodded for him to continue.

After they both ordered coffee, John continued. "Laura has gone for good." He took a deep breath and smiled broadly. "I know I should be devastated, but I am so relieved that I can't stop smiling."

Seeing the confused look on Tina's face, he went on more slowly. "She left the country with some man she met in the hospital. They are in Greece. She filed for divorce and says he is the love of her life, and they will be married as soon as possible."

John started to laugh in a manner Tina has never seen. He had always looked so sad; she had never even seen him smile. Her heart went out to him and in spite of herself; she started laughing as well. Both were thinking that this man in Greece had no idea what he was getting into.

John looked deep into Tina's eyes and took her hand. "I know I shouldn't say this, but my first reaction was to thank God. I could never have left her in the shape she was in, but I think it might have destroyed me to go on any longer the way it was. The only thing that has kept me going was our talks. Thank you! Thank you! Thank you!

Tina's heart was his in that moment. They were married one week after his divorce was final.

The ethical boundary was a gray area, since John Smith was never her client. Yet Tina felt she could no longer hold her head up in the community. She gave up her license to practice psychology, took a course in acupressure, and had never regretted her decision.

TINA AND DEIRDRE

Deirdre Warren had met Tina Angelino at a conference ten years before. They'd both discussed the need to have a peer therapist to process issues and maintain equilibrium. Nevertheless, both agreed that they had never met anyone they felt comfortable enough to share their cases and feelings.

They knew that Chad did this sort of work frequently and had a group of adoring followers who hung on his every word. Both Tina and Deirdre, however, vehemently agreed that they did not trust him. As they were both deeply intuitive, they based their feelings, not always on fact, but on a visceral feeling that they could not shake.

They began meeting on a monthly basis, and talked about their cases, their lives, their philosophies, and formed a bond that stood the test of scandal and the loss of their reputations.

Tina shared her concern about the growing attachment to the husband of one of her clients. Deirdre cautioned her and suggested transferring the client, but Tina felt that she could not abandon the couple until they could achieve some stability in their lives.

Tina, in turn, cautioned Deirdre about Jack Stiles. While most were mesmerized by Jack, Tina's sixth sense warned her that Stiles was not sincere. She even compared him to Chad.

Deirdre's red flags were raised with each warning from Tina, but she didn't know how to address her concerns with Jack. Each time she questioned him about inconsistencies or pointed out potential ethical boundaries, he would turn it around and point out how Deirdre's trust issues were caused by Robert, her former husband. She needed to learn to trust, he kept repeating.

When Jack was arrested, Tina was one of the few friends and colleagues who never believed that Deirdre was his co-conspirator.

Likewise, Deirdre stood solidly by Tina during her crisis of conscience. Deirdre felt that Tina should have fought to maintain her license, but supported her friend in her decision. When Tina became an acupressure specialist, Deirdre was her first client. The sessions were usually a mixture of acupressure, personal discussion, laughter, therapy, and lots of coffee.

Tina refused to accept payment for these sessions. After a long and heated dispute, and despite the resistance, Deirdre, blurring an ethical boundary, paid her in cash, leaving an envelope on the coffee table. Tina finally gave up and accepted the payment; however, she never told Deirdre that she put the money in a fund that she had started for an abused women's shelter. While Laura, John's wife, had not been abused as she'd claimed, many women were, and felt helpless to leave without a safe retreat. Tina felt a powerful need to provide a safe harbor for these women.

Her father was a strong Italian husband who had very traditional views about marriage and relationships. Tina had never seen her father raise his hand to anyone, especially not her mother, but there was a deep sense that all was not as perfect as her mother claimed.

Tina's mother swore that her husband was a saint and the best husband any woman could hope for. Yet there were times when she looked at him with fear in her eyes. Her daughter sensed that fear, but never had the courage to challenge her father.

It was only after she'd moved away that she began to question his behavior. There was nothing overt, but he would belittle without name-calling. He never actually said his wife was stupid, but would imply with small patronizing comments. Her mother seldom questioned or challenged her husband, but on the few occasions, Tina could see the flash of warning coming from her father.

Tina, herself, always did as she was told until leaving for college. It was then that she realized that relationships did not need to be so one-sided and controlled. Her desire to understand more and to change her own environment prompted her to go into the field that would help her learn about the many *whys* of behavior. Never abandoning her faith, however, Tina prayed frequently for Deirdre's safety and well-being.

TINA AND DEIRDRE

The minute Deirdre entered Tina's home, she felt wrapped in a cocoon of soothing peace and harmony. Candles burned on every table, a soft scent filled the room. The fragrance of the candles blended intoxicatingly with the huge plate of chocolate chip cookies and freshly brewed coffee. Many would think that Tina would prefer herbal teas, but like her friend, she had a penchant for good ground coffee, the stronger the better. Without speaking, she poured the coffee into one of her *View* mugs. Unlike Deirdre who limited her collection to the one mug, Tina had the entire set from each season. Hugging Tina, Deirdre breathed in the soothing energy her friend and colleague always emitted.

Just looking at her friend, Tina could see the tension radiating from Deirdre. Finally, she asked the question that had been worrying her.

"Do you think Jack will contact you?"

"I think he has already." Deirdre showed Tina the notes left on her front step. "Karol wants me to buy a gun."

Tina and Deirdre both shivered at the thought of bringing such a weapon into their homes.

"I can't tell you what to do. You need to follow your conscience on this one, Dee, but a gun?"

"I know. I feel the same way. I am not sure I could use it if I had it, but Karol thinks I should do everything I can to protect myself from Jack."

Tina shook her head. "I have a bad feeling about this, Dee. Are you convinced it is Jack? You know you have worked with some very disturbed people. We both have."

"It's Jack. I know it. Look how far he went. Hawke could have..."

Tina put her arms around her friend as they both recalled the horror Deirdre had gone through. They were both amazed that Hawke never carried out his purpose.

"Dee, I trust you on this. You will make the right decision."

Deirdre smiled at her friend. "Being with you always makes me feel better.

Taking a deep breath, Deirdre continued in a hesitant voice.

"There is something else I need to run by you. I can't give you details. I probably am violating confidentiality by discussing this at all, but I am so worried, and I need your take on an ethical issue."

"You are asking me? I am the last person you should trust with an ethical issue."

"Tina, stop. You are the most decent person I know, and in spite of everything, the most ethical. I trust you not to share this with anyone, and I trust your judgment." Tina merely nodded, and Deirdre continued.

"I have a client who has entered into a financial arrangement as a companion."

"You mean prostitution?"

"Well, not technically, but, yes, I guess you could call it that."

"Dee, you have had cases like this before. What makes this one so different?"

"Yes, but the ones I have worked with are mostly young college students who are making money to pay for their education. They have all seen it as the means to an end and take precautions. This one is very different."

"In what way?"

"First of all, she is much older. She has never done anything like this before, but is in an extreme financial bind. We naturally discussed ways to deal with the finances, but she has exhausted everything. She needs money, a lot of it, soon. I can't tell you much more than that, but she is definitely desperate."

"What is your issue, Dee?"

"I feel a responsibility to stop her from doing this, to talk her out of it, but it seems judgmental. Tina, I am afraid for her."

"Well, Dee, you know the last thing she needs from you is judgment. She needs your support. This does not qualify as a duty to warn, so you can't breech confidentiality. It seems that you need to just stay connected so that she has someone to help her process her feelings about this. If you seem in the least judgmental, she will cut you off."

"Yes, I know, I know, and I don't know why I feel differently about this one, but it just seems like a disastrous move for her. Not just physically dangerous, but I am not sure she can live with her decision emotionally. I truly fear for this woman, Tina."

Tina warmed her friend's coffee and took her hand.

"They don't always do what we think is best for them, Dee. The only thing you can do is give her the unconditional acceptance she needs. However, you can point out the risk factors. But I am sure you have already done that. Just don't allow the stressors you are under now cloud your judgment."

"I know, I have thought of that myself, and, yes, we have discussed the risk factors many times. She is determined that this is her only choice. I try not to take my cases home with me, but I have to admit that this one has been keeping me awake."

Deirdre sighed. "Unfortunately, I need to go. I just needed to spend some time with you. You always manage to help me see things in a fresh perspective. I'll call you soon."

"Dee, please take care."

"I will, you as well."

"And, Dee, someday soon we need to talk about your mother."

Deirdre shook her head and got into her car. As her friend drove away, Antoinette Marie Angelina-Smith, stood watching the car for many minutes before she turned back to her home with a worried expression. This was not going to end well.

DEIRDRE

Deirdre wished she had never told Tina about her mother. No one knew what life had been for her growing up, not even her x-husband, Robert or her friend, Karol. Something about Tina made people want to open up to her. Deirdre knew that Tina periodically opened that door in hopes that she would talk more about her mother, but it was always just too painful.

Her first memories were actually of her grandmother whom she called Nana. As a small child Deirdre had terrible ear aches. Her Nana would rock her and sing to her until she was able to fall asleep. When they eventually removed her tonsils, it was her Nana who spooned soothing ice cream into her mouth until she was able to eat something more solid. With Nana, Deirdre felt safe.

Occasionally, her mother would show up without warning. She was so beautiful and warm, Deirdre was always happy to see her. She could tell, however, that Nana was not always so pleased to see her daughter. Deirdre could hear them argue late at night, but Nana always gave in, and her mother would take Deirdre away with her.

At first it was wonderful being with her mother. She was so bubbly and fun. She bought her presents and took her to the movies and out for ice cream. But then her mother would become restless. She would put on her makeup, singing along with the radio. Then she would put Deirdre to bed and promise to be home soon.

It was always late at night when she returned, sometimes not until morning. Deirdre became terrified of the dark and would get up and turn all of the lights on, hugging her favorite doll. She talked to the doll throughout the night and kept reassuring her that it would be okay.

One night, the power went out during a severe electrical storm. Deirdre was hysterical, crying convulsively until a neighbor came and took her home, leaving a note for her mother. The neighbor never said anything derogatory about Deirdre's mother, but she could tell the woman was not friendly when she was picked up the next morning.

Sometimes, her mother would not return for days, leaving Deirdre to eat mayonnaise and mustard out of a jar or whatever else she could find in the cabinets. After a few days, her Nana would show up and take her home. Deirdre never knew how Nana discovered that her mother had left, but she always seemed to show up just when she was needed most. Perhaps the neighbors or her mother called. Nevertheless, Deirdre was always happy to see Nana. With Nana she felt safe.

The times with Nana grew longer. Nana would sew clothes for her favorite doll. On Sundays, they would read the funnies together. Deirdre would pretend to read long before she knew the words. She often thought that this was where she developed the love of reading.

Deirdre had mixed feelings when her mother finally showed up again. In spite of the bad times, she loved her mother. She was the most beautiful woman she had ever seen, and she had a mesmerizing singing voice.

As she got older, the times with her mother grew more difficult. She never knew whether her mother would be there when she returned from school or in what condition. Sometimes she would be drunk, and Deirdre would try to sober her up, but that angered her, and she would hit Deirdre with whatever object she could reach and call her names until she passed out. When she woke, she was always warm and loving, but it was the not knowing that was so hard for Deirdre.

She knew her mother wasn't a bad person, and Deirdre did love her deeply. She was just very troubled. On numerous occasions, Deirdre had to bandage her mother's wrists after she had cut herself. At first she called an ambulance and was terrified her mother would die. Then she discovered that her mother wasn't actually trying to die; she just wanted attention. When Deirdre wanted to go out with friends or spend time doing her homework and her mother wanted her to talk or watch TV with her or go out to the movies, she would find a way to capture her daughter's attention.

Deirdre never brought friends home because her mother would inevitably embarrass her in some way. Deirdre's mother wanted to be their friend and would try to do the latest dance with them or show off. The kids would laugh at her, and Deirdre felt she needed to defend her. She lost a lot of friends that way.

No matter how difficult the night was, the next day was always school. Sometimes her clothes were dirty and wrinkled, and the kids would laugh at her, but nevertheless, Deirdre felt safe in school. Getting good grades made her feel like everything was okay. Someday she knew she would go to college and be able to take care of herself. She would never feel helpless again.

Wen her mother died, Deirdre felt sad, but she also felt relieved. How can you love someone that you dislike so intensely? How can you hurt someone that you love? Yet both those things were true. She knew that her mother loved her in spite of everything, and she loved her, but living with Nana made her feel safe.

Everyone says that people go into the field of psychology in order to understand their own childhood. Deirdre thought that was probably true because she always wanted to understand people like her mother. Could someone have made a difference; have helped her mother, or her?

Deirdre was thankful that her Nana was able to be with her long enough to see h er graduate from college. That period of time with Nana gave her the courage she needed to continue her education and get that final degree that allowed her to do the work she always wanted to do.

DEIRDRE

Deirdre's father, Hale Warren, did some sort of undefined work in law enforcement that took him away for long periods of time. Everyone assumed it was his constant absence that was responsible for the divorce. Deirdre never asked, but thought it was more likely just that her mother couldn't stay in one relationship for any length of time.

Her father wasn't completely absent from her life. He just wasn't around that much after the divorce. She could never remember her parents being together, although she would get occasional flashes of memory that seemed very warm and pleasant.

He wrote to her, very adult letters to a small child. He never seemed to be able to communicate on any other level. Nana would read the letters to her and try to interpret some of the comments. Several times a year, he stopped by for a visit, but never stayed more than a day or two.

When she was twelve, Deirdre's father asked her to spend some time with him during summer vacation. At first it was okay. He would take her out to eat, and they would go to the movies, usually Westerns or cops and robbers.

He was never a warm and fuzzy person. He didn't hug her or kiss her like some dads did with their daughters, but he tried hard to talk to her about things that interested her. They sometimes played cards and would watch TV together. She made him coffee. He actually laughed at her the first time she did that, but she became very good at it.

He was supposed to be off duty that entire month, but there always seemed to be some issue that called him away. He would apologize for having to leave and promise another outing soon. After a while though, she found herself alone a lot during that month.

Toward the end of the visit, a man, whom her father was instrumental in arresting and convicting, escaped from prison. He vowed to get even with her father. Naturally, there was a manhunt to find him and also a concern that he would target Hale's daughter.

Deirdre remembered crouching down in her bed as searchlights flooded the windows. The house was surrounded with armed men, ostensibly to keep her safe. Yet no one thought that what a twelve-year-old girl needed most was someone to hug her and tell her it would be okay.

Sometimes after she went to bed, Deirdre's father and his friends would play cards in the kitchen until late at night. She could hear them talking. Curious, as most children are, she listened intently.

"Hale, doesn't it bother you that you turned in one of your own?"

At first, the silence crackled with tension. People seldom confronted her father. He never raised his voice but spoke in a deep, grim manner that broached no argument.

"Because there is nothing I hate more than a dirty cop. Deal the cards."

The game continued in silence. The question was never asked again.

The next day, while eating breakfast of toast with peanut butter, Deirdre asked her father, "Daddy, why do you have to go away so much and work with bad people?"

He put down his toast, looked into her eyes, and thought for a moment, "Because, Dee, the world is full of evil, making good people live in fear. I want to make the world clean. I want to make it safe."

He picked up and sat her on his knee, something he seldom did. "Whatever you do in this life, make it count. Do something that has meaning, something that leaves the world a cleaner place."

"I will, Daddy, I promise."

Hale Warren was killed in the line of duty just two months later. Deirdre knew that she would make the world a safer place, she just wasn't sure how.

DEIRDRE

Deirdre loved her work, but maintaining objectivity had always been one area of difficulty. She'd managed to follow the ethical rules about not taking gifts or developing friendships, but relational boundaries involving caring became more confusing to her. She couldn't help worrying about her clients and wondered if she could do more to help them.

Clearly she'd blurred a boundary with Jack, trusting him in spite of her inner warnings, which allowed him to have access to her clients. Recognizing that error and paying for it dearly instilled a diligence in her about maintaining appropriate boundaries. Deirdre swore to herself that she would always enforce healthy boundaries. Yet sometimes a client would reach through that professional wall, becoming an emotional concern.

Such was the case with Marcia. Deirdre realized that her level of concern was blurring her objectivity. Perhaps she should refer Marcia to another therapist? That was probably the professional thing to do. Yet Deirdre didn't feel that she was able to abandon Marcia at this point in her life. Was she helping Marcia, however, or doing an injustice by being so involved? The therapeutic relationship can be very complicated.

MARCIA

Marcia Gomez had cared for her mother, Claire, for the past ten years, since she had been diagnosed with early Alzheimer's. At first, the money left by her father seemed more than enough to pay for her mother's care in the facility where she and her father placed her lovingly shortly before his death. Marcia believed that the stress of having to put his beloved wife in a long-term care facility brought on the massive heart attack.

Marcia and her father had tried to care for Claire in the beginning by taking shifts watching her and also hiring caretakers to come into the home when they could not be there. In the long run, it was not enough. She slipped out of the house late at night when they were both asleep and was found walking near the interstate. Fortunately, she was not hurt, but Marcia and her father were confronted with the risks of keeping Claire at home.

Her parents had been together since high school, sweethearts until the end. Her father's grief was palpable when he was forced to leave his wife for the first time in her new *home*.

Marcia's father left a trust to be executed by his daughter for the care of her mother. He seemed to know that he would not be there much longer. Marcia had a good job in banking; she made an excellent income. Her father's trust paid for her mother's care. Ironically, in spite of the disease which damaged her mind, Claire remained healthy and alive. The money, which had seemed plentiful, began to appear as though it would not provide for her care indefinitely. Marcia began to worry.

She was approached many times in the banking industry by those who talked about high-yield investments. Marcia had felt these investments to be much too risky and had always avoided them. Now she began to think about increasing her own 401 and her mother's trust through such a group of investments. Not surprisingly, the money evaporated, leaving Marcia frantic about how she would maintain her mother's care and her own livelihood.

She sold the family home, putting that into the trust account, and moved into a small apartment. She put the majority of her income into the trust account to attempt to replenish the money lost. In spite of her lifelong fear of credit card debt, Marcia began to use the cards to pay her own bills, trying to replace the money lost. She took out loans, putting the money into the account. The debt mounted, and the money still was not enough to keep her mother for more than another year.

Insomnia became a nightly event. Marcia tried sleeping pills, but felt sick the next day. She began sleeping only a few hours each night. Not a big TV watcher, Marcia spent her wee hours surfing the net. During one of these nights, she discovered a Web site that advertised *arranged companions*. She started to delete it and move on, but then began to read. Gentlemen would pay a monthly allowance to a woman to serve as his companion. Sex was not mentioned, however it was implied. The idea was that a man wanted a woman to take to events, spend time with, but not have to worry about a commitment or complications. Most were probably married, but that was not mentioned.

Marcia had never married; she considered herself an old maid. She was over forty and not a raving beauty. Although she was not unattractive, she had never spent a lot of time or money on her appearance. Impulsively, she responded to a gentleman. He was older, about fifty or so, and somewhat overweight. He had posted his picture. They chatted online, and he asked her to send a picture.

Marcia went out that weekend and got a quick makeover. Then she had a picture taken that she thought was reasonably attractive and sent it the next night. He must have thought it was okay as he asked to meet her. She quickly agreed, but feeling weighted down by the enormity of this move, she called to schedule an appointment with her therapist, Dr. Deirdre Warren. She had been seeing Dr. Warren since her father's death, trying to cope with her grief and anxiety over her mother's care.

Dr. Warren was not judgmental about Marcia's decision, but she could tell the doctor was concerned. The talked a lot about safety precautions, health issues, and so forth. The entire time, Marcia could tell that Dr.

Warren did not want her to go through with this. They had long exhausted financial alternatives, so they were at a stalemate. Marcia had her first *date* that night.

MARCIA

The minute she met Howard, her anxiety level diminished considerably. He was short, slightly overweight, with a round face that smiled from the eyes on out. He seemed even more nervous that she, which helped a lot.

He took her out to dinner and talked, laughing nervously from time to time. He agreed to give her some money to help her out, but made no sexual overtures. After dinner, he walked her to her car, handed out an envelope with money, kissed her on the cheek, and promised to call.

Marcia drove home believing that things would be all right after all. These men just wanted some companionship. Then there was Charles.

Charles was just the opposite of Howard. He was tall, extremely handsome, and seemed very well educated. Marcia couldn't help but wonder why he was on the Web site. He could date anyone he wished.

Dinner was elegant with lots of wine that he ordered by name and year, explaining that he was a collector of fine wines. He asked her very little about herself, which was fine with Marcia, and talked a lot about his accomplishments. He had just built a new home in the country, which he was in the process of decorating. He would love to show it to her.

After dinner, they got into his car, one she had never seen before (but clearly expensive), and drove to his new house. After showing her around, he proceeded to open a bottle from his new wine collection. She was still a bit tipsy from the restaurant but didn't want to offend him by declining.

Somewhere during the first few sips of wine, the atmosphere changed. She could actually feel a charge and a smell. Does evil have a smell? His face hardened and changed, the smile gone. Marcia began to feel afraid.

"It is time." He stood up and took her hand firmly leading her down the hall toward the bedroom.

The room was brightly lighted but cold, very much unlike the rest of the house. He pushed her back on the bed and began removing her clothes.

"But I thought." She stammered.

"You thought what, honey? That I was going to give you a pile of money for your charming company? You aren't that charming, and a bit over the hill for this. You should be flattered I didn't walk out in the first five minutes."

Some deep instinct warned her that resisting would be futile, and could even get her hurt. She wasn't convinced he wouldn't hurt her anyway. So she closed her eyes and wished it to end soon.

Unfortunately, it seemed to go on for hours. He made no effort toward lubrication and proceeded to violate her in as many ways as possible. The pain had become a part of her existence, inseparable from her body and mind, as she tried desperately to pray for forgiveness and an end to the whole experience.

Without warning, it was over. He threw her clothes at her and walked out of the room, wordless. When she emerged from the bedroom, he was tossing down the rest of his wine. Grabbing his car keys, he gestured her toward the door and into his car.

She was terrified that he would kill her and dump her body in the woods. When the car stopped abruptly, she was relieved to see her car. Pushing a button to open the passenger side, he wordlessly gestured for her to get out. He was clearly finished with her.

Marcia grabbed her pocketbook and fled to her car, locking the doors the moment she entered. Sobbing hysterically, she vomited into her pocketbook until there was nothing left in her stomach. It was several hours before she was able to stop sobbing and drive home.

After showering for over an hour in an attempt to wash away her humiliation and fear, she threw on her warmest and oldest sweat suit and crawled into bed. Curing into a tight ball, she fell into a dark and fitful sleep.

It was barely dawn when she woke up the next morning. Fortunately, it was the weekend, and she didn't need to go into work. There were bruises all over her body, and she couldn't stop shivering. She knew there was no way she would have been able to work that day.

The queasy knot in her stomach resisted any thought of food or even coffee. She went immediately to her computer, taking down her profile page from the Web site. She never wanted to look at that site again.

Putting her purse in the sink, she began to remove the items she needed to save before tossing the vomit-soaked item. It was then she noticed the envelop filled with money. Furiously, she threw the envelop into the trash, washing off her wallet and identification cards. Picking up the trash bag, she carried it out to the Dumpster. At the last moment, however, she took the envelop out of the bag.

Returning to her kitchen, she took out the money and began to wash it in warm water, laying it out on the counter to dry. It was the hardest money she'd ever earned.

MIKE

Mike threw down the notes in a rage. "Dammit, Dee, why didn't you tell me this was going on. I'll kill that son of a bitch!"

Deirdre grabbed Mike's arm and tried to calm him down. "We aren't even sure it was Jack. It could have been an irate client. It could be a joke."

"Some joke! Did you call the police?"

"Of course, but they can't really do anything. They took the notes, but the only prints were mine. We just have to wait until he makes a move of some sort."

"Some sort? You mean if he kills you?"

Suddenly, Mike stopped pacing and crushed Deirdre in his arms. "What if something happened to you, and I couldn't stop it?"

He pulled her down next to him on the sofa. "I love you, Dee. I have for a long time, but I didn't realize just how deeply until I thought I could lose you."

Deirdre felt the tears streaming down her face.

"Mike, I love you, too, but you won't lose me. Jack is a coward. I know him. He is just trying to scare me. One appearance, one phone call, and I can have him violated and put back in prison. Please, Mike, don't worry."

"Well, I'm canceling my next trip. I won't leave you alone. Maybe I should move in here."

"We talked about that. We want to do this right. We don't want anyone to be able to muddy our love in any way. Besides, I think that might upset Emily."

"Are you kidding? Emily loves you. She told me so. She is happy for us."

"Yes, I agree, but she is still very sensitive. I think we need to wait. Go on your trip, Mike. I can have Karol stay here if it makes you feel better, or even Emily might want to stay." She shook her head, "No, on second thought, I don't want Emily to know about this just yet."

"You must be seeing something in Emily that I don't see. I know she had some problems as a teenager, but I never thought she was that fragile."

"Maybe you're right, Mike. I hope so. It's just something I feel."

Deirdre snuggled down in Mike's arms. "Let's just enjoy each other for tonight."

"You got it." Mike pulled her up next to him and covered her soft mouth with his, and they both forgot everything except each other.

ROBERT

Those who didn't know Deirdre thought she was either very stupid or equally guilty for having ever been involved with Jack Stiles. What could she have been thinking? Even Karol, who knew her best, had difficulty wrapping her mind around the conflict between the level-headed friend and the woman who allowed this man to destroy her life.

She'd never really talked about Robert, not even to Karol or Tina. Often when people would comment about how damaging Jack had been to her Deirdre thought, if only they knew just how much worse Robert had been.

Of course, everyone knew that she had divorced Robert after nearly twenty years of marriage. Karol was the only one who knew that she had taken literally nothing with her, as she'd helped her move into a small apartment with no furniture and a set of Kmart pots and pans. For weeks, Deirdre slept on a small futon that had been in her office. She also had a tiny television and an old stereo that she managed to hook up herself. Deirdre never complained, just kept working and saving her money, buying only the basics to survive. There were no paintings on the walls, and she ate popcorn most nights for dinner.

Saving every cent, Deirdre eventually was able to buy the small townhome that she loved. Karol also knew the pride Deirdre took in each purchase until the home was hers—and hers alone.

What no one knew was how much damage Robert had done to her. On the surface, he was the perfect husband and wonderful provider. He was handsome, successful, and charming in public. Everyone loved Robert and all were shocked when Deirdre left him with no warning.

No, there had been no bruises, no broken bones, and no trips to the emergency room to justify her fear of him. The scars he left were deep and intensely emotional.

The first few years were wonderful. Robert loved the fact that his wife was getting her degree and supported her completely. After graduation, he was the one who insisted that she continue her education to obtain her master's degree in psychology.

Things seemed to change following that second graduation, though. He was irritated a lot about small things, constantly criticizing her colleagues, calling them *ivory-tower eggheads*. He also began to throw wild fits of jealousy. Who was she laughing with on the phone? Why was she late coming home?

She'd begun to work for a small counseling practice and often got home later than she'd planned. Even though he was frequently late himself, Robert would be furious when she failed to be there when he came home.

The first time she thought he might actually hit her was the night she was two hours late working with a colleague regarding a particularly difficult client. She'd left him a note saying that they would have steaks, salad, and wine at seven. She didn't make it home until after nine, but had called twice to let him know she was tied up and would get there as soon as possible.

When she arrived, he'd burned the steaks and thrown them in the trash. He was drinking the wine and had obviously had several glasses.

I will not be your househusband, he raged. *It is your job to take care of the house, my house that I paid for. I will not sit around waiting while you are screwing your clients or your partners.*

His eyes were wild, his face red with rage. She thought he might actually hit her then. In panic, the thoughts raced through her mind. What could she do? Call the police? Get help? Who could she call?

It was then she realized that she had few friends other than the ones Robert had approved—his friends. He didn't hit her though. He finished the wine and went to bed. After that, he took pleasure in inflicting small hurts.

His favorite pain was over dinner in a restaurant. Robert knew how much Deirdre hated public embarrassment.

The evening began amicably. They chatted and laughed, and then some small things set him off—another diner recognized her and said hello, a waiter smiled at her.

His eyes changed. She could almost feel the air becoming menacing around her, and she knew it was coming. His voice would get louder. He would complain to the waiter about the food or service. He waited for her reaction, wanting to feel pain.

She always tried to get through it without showing any emotion. She knew though that until she revealed her hurt, he would not let up. Often she excused herself to the ladies' room and tried to gain some composure. Sometimes she would just sit at the table, silently, as the tears streamed down her face. She prayed no one would notice.

He also reminded her frequently that he paid the bills and he owned the house and the furniture She was not to move things around without his permission. He would leave little Post-it notes on the faucets or lamps telling her they needed polishing. He refused to hire a cleaning service, insisting she do the cleaning herself. It was her job, he reminded her; however, he was never satisfied, complaining constantly.

It was when she defended the dissertation for her PhD that she finally accepted that she did not have a marriage. He colleagues were waiting at the office with a bottle of champagne. They were happy for her, and she was feeling exhilarated.

She called Robert, and he said they would celebrate that evening. He actually sounded pleased for her. Perhaps this would be a good night after all.

When she arrived home, he was still at work, so she showered and put on something new that she'd been saving for a special occasion. He's probably made a reservation at someplace fancy.

Three hours later, he walked in the door, and she knew this would not be a good night after all.

"You're dressed up. Oh, right the dissertation." He kissed her briefly and frowned when he noticed the faint smell of champagne on her breath. "I guess you started celebrating without me."

Robert, that was hours ago, I had one glass of champagne with my coworkers. We were celebrating.

When he turned around, she could see the look of disgust on his face.

"Oh, of course, you were with that pack of pseudo-intellectuals. You would rather celebrate with them. Which one are you screwing? Or is it all of them?"

Deirdre was surprised that she wasn't angry or upset, just resigned. She grabbed her purse and keys, left the house, and stayed in a hotel that night. The next day, while he was at work, she packed a suitcase, took a box of books and her laptop, and left the house for good.

Robert, called her cell phone in a fury.

"You bitch. I will ruin you. You won't get a cent from me. I will tell everyone what a whore you are. When I'm through with you, you wont have anything but the clothes on your back,."

She actually laughed, which enraged him even more.

"I don't want your money, Robert, I never have. Good-bye."

She knew she'd done t he right thing, but her confidence was shattered. For an entire year, she worked every hour she could, then went home and cried herself to sleep. People suggested she get out, meet new people. She even went to a happy hour one afternoon. She walked briskly around the bar, once, feeling all the eyes on her, and then out the door. This was not going to be for her.

Work was the only time she felt comfortable. Strange people made her anxious unless they were clients. Who would ever want to be with her? She was over the hill, unattractive, unlovable, a failure. Life held no promise for her. Then she met Jack. She was obviously ripe for the picking.

DEIRDRE

Tonight! He was coming for her tonight. Deirdre woke with the certainly that this would b e the night that he tried to kill her. She thought she should be afraid, but and eerie calm came over her at the realization that tonight it would be over at last. It would all end.

There were many loose ends that needed to be completed, and Deirdre spend the day finishing notes and paperwork. She also finalized her will and e-mailed it to her attorney for safekeeping—just in case.

As the day wore on and the afternoon shadows lengthened, Deirdre felt a growing excitement. It wasn't fear, but anticipation. She took a long relaxing shower, washed her hair, taking her time. She dressed in a running suit, but kept her on the slippers. No need for shoes when targeted for death. A hysterical bubble of laughter burst from her mouth.

Keep it together, Deirdre.

As dusk fell, she began the preparations for what was to come. She turned off her phone, sending the calls directly to voice mail. She wanted none of her loved ones to be involved. She wanted to call Hawke, but somehow believed he already knew what she wanted to tell him. As much as she ached for contact with Mike, she didn't dare involved him or Karol. They would both be put to risk if they tried to interfere. No, she needed to do this on her own.

The evening darkened from gray to black. She dared another look out the window before lowering the shades. She could feel the evil.

Does evil have a presence?

She knew it was near, nonetheless.

Walking from room to room, Deirdre pulled all the drapes closed, leaving one lamp on in her bedroom. Taking the box down, once more, from its resting place, she removed the black gun from its case and loaded the clip as she was taught by Karol.

"You and me," she said to the object. "It's up to us."

Deirdre allowed herself one small glass of white wine. After disengaging the alarm, she carried the wine to her favorite chair in the living room, facing the door. She felt Pax jump on the back of the chair, purring softly. The warmth of the cat and the soft sound combined with the wine soothed her. The revolver rested in her lap, and she stroked it periodically. A voice deep inside rumbled now and then.

Violence is not the answer.

As she turned off the lights, Deirdre quieted the voice. *I've tried everything else. Shut up!*

Shadows fell on the door and the chair next to it. Somehow she knew he would come through the front door. He was that brazen. No sneaking through the basement for him. Calmly, she watched the door and waited for him to come.

HAWKE

Hawke waited in the bushes, ignoring his growing need to empty his bladder, ignoring the rumble in his stomach.

He was focused on one thing.

Evil was coming.

It had been dark for hours. He couldn't see his watch but knew it was well after midnight. Then he saw it. A shadow moved across the lawn and into the side of the house. He could hear its breathing, almost felling its breath. Evil was here. He waited a few more moments before he saw the second shadow close behind.

He'd seen the lights go out and knew she was waiting for Jack. Did she have the courage to use the gun?

No, not courage, he knew she had that. Did she have the ability to take another life, even it protection of her own? That, he questioned.

It would not be long now. Quick as a cat, he moved toward the house, his knife at the ready—just in case.

EMILY

Deirdre eyes had become accustomed to the dark, and she was able to clearly see the door as it slowly opened and the shadowy figure entered. She reached for the gun, but suddenly heard and felt the shot as the light snapped on across from her.

She blinked and looked across the room toward the light. Emily!

"What are you doing here? It's not safe. You need to get out of here, Jack is…"

Then she noticed the gun in Emily's hand. It was pointed upward toward the ceiling. Finally, Deirdre realized the gun was not aimed at her.

"I don't understand, Emily. What?"

Emily began to laugh, but her voice sounded different, not like her at all.

"Did you really think I would let you take my daddy from me you bitch?"

Realization began to surface as Deirdre's hand tightened on the gun in her lap.

"It's been you all along. I thought Jack…"

"I don't know anything about this Jack you keep talking about, but yes, it's me. I have hated you since the moment Daddy introduced you. I knew what you wanted.

You wanted to take him from me. All that pretending. Trying to act like you actually cared about me. Hah! I could see through you all along.

"No, Emily, don't do this. You need help. Let me help you. We can do this together. You don't have to do this."

"Shut up, you lying bitch. The only thing I want you to do is die. The first shot was just to wake you up. This one will do the job." Emily raised the gun as Deridre lifted her own revolver. Her hand shook, and tears streamed down her face. Dropping the gun into her lap, she muttered to herself, "I can't do this. It's not her fault."

She closed her eyes as the second shot rang out.

Where was the pain? Was she dead? She looked up as Karol and Hawke were holding Emily's arms. Pax's furry, blood-soaked body lay in her lap where she had fallen from her perch behind Deirdre's head. The second shot had just missed her, but had killed her beloved friend.

Karol had reached Emily first and grabbed the gun. Hawke ran in right behind her, tying her hands.

"Christ, Dee," Karol cried. "She just missed you. Why didn't you use the gun?"

"Pax, oh no, not Pax." Deirdre kept repeating.

"I am sorry about the cat, Dee, but it could have been you."

"The cops will be here any minute," Hawke knelt in front of Deirdre. " I have to go."

Deirdre smiled at her very unusual old friend. "Yes, go. We'll talk later."

Karol finished tying Emily to the chair and turned to face her friend. "Hawke warned me she was coming. He's been watching her all along. Jack got his hooks into her. He's been calling Scotty. Between him and Chad, they were convincing Emily to get rid of you before you married her father."

"Jack?"

"Oh, he's gone. Took off yesterday. Hawke wanted to go after him, but couldn't leave you until we stopped Emily. He'll find him eventually though. God help Jack when he does."

Deirdre's arms were covered in blood as she cradled her cat. She knew her Pax was gone, but she couldn't let go.

They both turned to Emily as she began sobbing, "Daddy, Daddy, where are you?"

Karol and Deirdre looked at each other. Someone had to tell Mike.

The sirens grew louder.

EPILOGUE

Deirdre hasn't seen Mike since the night Emily was arrested. He had been heavily involved with Emily's legal issues and obtaining appropriate psychiatric care for his daughter. Deirdre had agreed not to press charges if Emily would get professional help. Nevertheless, the legal ramifications were far from over. So when he called to say he wanted to see her, Deirdre was both happy and apprehensive.

The moment she saw Mike, Deirdre knew her fears were justified. He kissed her briefly but backed away immediately, not holding her the way he always did following a kiss. She kept trying to look at him, but he avoided eye contact. She could see the pain and conflict in his face.

"This isn't your fault, Mike."

""She's my daughter. She tried to kill you. She killed your cat. My God!"

Deirdre winced with the memory. She still grieved with the loss of her precious pet. She'd wrapped Pax in her favorite blanket and buried her in the backyard with her well-chewed toy mouse. Visiting her tiny grave every day, she talked to the cat, assuring her that she would never be replaced. Not a day passed that she didn't wake expecting the cat to be sitting on the pillow beside her.

"She's sick, Mike. As hurt as I am, I can't blame her." She watched Mike intently for a moment, then continued. "There's something else, isn't there?"

Mike turned away from her, his shoulder's slumping. When he turned to look at her, the pain radiated from his face. It was then that Deirdre knew it was over.

"She needs me now, Dee. I can't abandon her. Not again."

"You've never abandoned her."

"She doesn't know that. Deep down, she thinks she is alone. Dee, I don't know how long this will take, but I have to be there for her."

Deirdre sighed. "I know, Mike, I understand. Take as long as you need. I'll be here."

"No, Dee, I can't ask that. I just don't know."

"So it's over then?

Mike ran his hands through his hair, shaking his head. Sliding the ring from her finger, Deirdre took Mike's hand and closed it around the diamond.

He looked at her briefly, his eyes bright with tears, his face taut with pain. "I have to go." He turned and walked briskly out the door without looking back.

For long minutes Deirdre stood watching the door as if expecting him to return. She knew he wouldn't. She felt empty. She lost Pax—and now Mike. No more tears left, just a very deep ache.

The words from a poem by Robert Frost ran through he mind.

> Of all the words of tongue and pen,
> the saddest are, it might have been.

She finally turned from the door, feeling defeated.

Taking a deep breath, she looked down where the ring had been.

"No," she said aloud. "I did the right thing."

AUTHOR'S NOTE

Although sociopaths give little thought to the morality of their actions, most of us struggle with the concept of right and wrong. Our concept of morality and ethics, however, varies. For many, it is based on rules, laws, or religious doctrine. Others, however, make their determination from a deep, intuitive feeling. Some might call it a sixth sense.

Jack and Chad were both the epitome of sociopaths, caring nothing for the welfare of others and enjoying the power of manipulation and destruction.

Hawke, while basically diagnosable as a sociopath (or psychopath) did have an inner sense of humanity, somehow changing his actions from evil to good at times.

Emily was an example of those whose hatred and desire to harm was born out of a psychological disorder. Her delusions convinced her that Deirdre was going to take her father away. Jack and Chad encouraged her hostility and manipulated her fears.

Karol's support of gun ownership came from her childhood experience and need for self-protection. Yet she was an advocate for gun control as she firmly believed that those who purchased guns do so legally and become trained in how to use them safely. While many might disagree with her philosophy, her intentions were honorable.

Mike is one of those extremely concrete individuals. Good and bad were obvious. He lived by his beliefs and wanted others to do the same. He is clearly one of the white hats.

Tina and Deirdre focused on their intuitive belief in right and wrong rather than rules and dogma. Tina realized that her emotions for her husband overruled her concern for the ethical standards of her profession; therefore, she chose to give up her career.

Deirdre, while believing in ethical standards, recognized that she had allowed her boundaries to be violated by Jack during their marriage. She dedicated her actions toward maintaining those standards. At the same time, her intuitive direction told her that Tina, who had crossed the ethical lines, was a loving and caring individual. She also recognized the malevolence behind Chad's grand demeanor and credentials.

These are many different people, with many different values. How do we determine right and wrong? It is not always obvious.

www.ingramcontent.com/pod-product-compliance
Lightning Source LLC
LaVergne TN
LVHW011721060526
838200LV00051B/2982